Gehrke

Annie Henry

and the
Redcoats

Adventures of the American Revolution Series

★ ★ ★ ★ ★ ★ ★ ★ ★ ★ ★ ★ ★ ★ ★ ★
ADVENTURES OF THE AMERICAN REVOLUTION
★ ★ ★ ★ ★ ★ ★ ★ ★ ★ ★ ★ ★ ★ ★ ★

Annie Henry

and the
Redcoats

Susan Olasky

CROSSWAY BOOKS • WHEATON, ILLINOIS
A DIVISION OF GOOD NEWS PUBLISHERS

Annie Henry and the Redcoats

Copyright © 1996 by Susan Olasky

Published by Crossway Books
        a division of Good News Publishers
        1300 Crescent Street
        Wheaton, Illinois 60187

Cover illustration: Tom LaPadula

First printing, 1996

Printed in the United States of America

Library of Congress Cataloging-in-Publication Data
Olasky, Susan.
    Annie Henry and the Redcoats / Susan Olasky.
       p.   cm. — (Adventures of the American Revolution ; bk. 4)
    Summary: In 1789, the year Annie Henry turns sixteen, her family moves to Leatherwood on the frontier and she ends up in Richmond, where she gets a close look at the Revolutionary War.
    ISBN 0-89107-908-4
    1. Henry, Annie—Juvenile fiction. 2. Henry, Patrick, 1736–1799—Juvenile fiction. [1. Henry, Annie—Fiction. 2. Henry, Patrick, 1736–1799—Fiction. 3. United States—History—Revolution, 1775–1783—Fiction.] I. Title. II. Series.
PZ7.0425Anr 1996
[Fic]—dc20   96-33031

04		03		02		01		00		99		98		97	
15	14	13	12	11	10	9	8	7	6	5	4	3	2

For
Mom and Dad

CONTENTS

A DANGEROUS JOURNEY

"I SURE WISH THAT BABY WOULD STOP CRYING," BETSY complained. "Why doesn't Dolly feed her?" She tucked a few stray pieces of hair back under her blue gingham sun bonnet and scowled at the howls coming from the wagon behind.

Next to her on the seat at the front of the big Conestoga wagon, her older sister Annie smiled. "At least we know the baby has good, strong lungs. She's been crying for the past hour and doesn't seem at all tired of it."

"But I'm tired of it," twelve-year-old Betsy grumbled under her breath.

Annie pulled her sister's bonnet down over her eyes, letting her own laughter drown out the younger girl's complaints. "I'll make you switch wagons if all you do is complain," she said. "Perhaps you should go sit with the cooking pots. They won't mind your grumbling."

Next to them on the seat, Joseph, one of Patrick Henry's many slaves, yawned. They had already been on the trail for two days, and he was use to listening to the girls' mild bickering. He wiped a handkerchief across his sweaty brow and pulled his tricornered hat lower over his eyes. The afternoon sun was bright.

"I don't know why we couldn't travel in a more comfortable coach," Betsy said as she vainly fanned herself. "It's hotter'n blazes. I can't hardly breathe."

"We couldn't bring a nice city coach out on this trail," Annie answered. "Just look at the ruts and rocks. Why, we'd never get to Leatherwood. Already it's going to take nearly seven days."

Betsy groaned. "Why couldn't Father have stayed in Richmond? Aunt Anne said he could make a fortune as a lawyer, and if Dolly keeps having babies, he'll need a fortune. I don't know why we have to go out to the frontier."

Annie closed her eyes and let the sun warm her face. Her own bonnet hung down her back, despite her sister's constant reminders that the sun would bring out unsightly freckles. At nearly sixteen, Annie was still small. Although not beautiful, she had lively gray eyes and a quick smile that was attractive. She wore her wiry dark hair in a plain style, away from her face, because she wouldn't spend hours every day having her hair styled, as many women did.

Letting the rhythm of the wagon lull her into near-sleep, she thought about the changes that were in store for her family. It wasn't easy to leave the luxury of the Governor's Palace for a house on the frontier. But that's what her father, the famous patriot Patrick Henry, had wanted.

He had always loved the land. From the time he had bought Scotchtown in Hanover County, he had dreamed about going farther west where the land was good and neighbors were far away. Politics and duty had kept him in the city. But now, having finished two terms as governor, he had sold Scotchtown and bought 16,000 acres in Henry County, Virginia, right on the frontier. She smiled as she thought about living in a county named after her own daddy.

It wouldn't be an easy life. After all, it was 1779, and the Revolutionary War still raged. For two years the British had been stirring up the Indians all along the frontier and encouraging them to raid the white settlements. Things were worse on the other side of the mountains, especially in Kentucky, but her father said that all settlers had to be constantly alert.

Annie's thoughts were interrupted by a yelp and the sound of hooves against the sun-baked ground. Sitting up, she caught sight of her nine-year-old brother Neddy charging toward the wagon on his pony.

"Whoa, Master Neddy," Joseph shouted as he steadied his own team of skittish horses. "Slow down before you cause an accident."

The sweating boy brought his horse under control.

"You can't get the horse all lathered up like that on a hot day like today," Annie scolded. "I don't know when we'll find water." She stopped scolding, though, when she saw the frightened look on his face.

"Something scare you?" Betsy teased. "Maybe Indians," she added. "You've been telling us you've seen Indians all day."

The boy blushed. "It wasn't Indians," he said. "It was a rattler, fatter than my fist. Lying smack in the middle of the trail. I thought at first it was dead, so I pulled up close. Then I heard the rattling. The snake raised its head and looked at me. Lightning didn't wait to see what would happen next. He just bolted out of there. Nearly knocked me from the saddle." The boy gulped for air as the words tumbled out of his mouth.

"A rattlesnake?" Annie looked skeptical. "I never have seen one. Are you sure it wasn't just an old grass snake?"

"Do you think I can't tell the difference?" the boy said scornfully. "I'll tell Father. Maybe he'll let me shoot it."

Without waiting to hear more from his sisters, the boy rode off in search of his father. Just finding him would be a job. There were ten wagons carrying household furnishings for Patrick Henry, his second wife, Dolly, and their new baby, also named Dolly. In addition, the caravan included Annie, Betsy, Neddy, and their older sister Patsy, all of them Patrick Henry's children from his first marriage. Patsy traveled with her husband, John Fontaine, and their three small children. The Henry household also included many slaves. Livestock brought up the rear of the caravan. There were cows, oxen, horses, and even pigs.

From her place in the first wagon, Betsy shuddered. "I don't like snakes," she said.

"Don't be silly," Annie admonished her. "A snake would have to have wings to get up on this old wagon."

For the next few minutes the girls were silent as the wagon bumped its way along the rocky trail. Next to them, Joseph pulled up on the reins. Annie saw that the trail led down to a creek about fifteen feet across, then resumed on the other side. Behind them, the other wagons creaked to a stop.

Joseph hopped down from his seat and helped the girls down. Annie stretched. She felt stiff from riding all day, and the tight corset that she wore under her dress bit into her side. "I'd give anything to be ten again," she whispered to Betsy.

But the younger girl shook her head scornfully. "Not me. I love looking all grown-up," she said, smoothing out her own hooped skirt.

Next to her sister, Annie felt rumpled and hot. Her dress hung limply at her side, while Betsy's looked cool and crisp. Though four years separated them, she sometimes felt Betsy was the older one.

While the horses and cattle were watered, the girls wandered back to the second wagon, where Dolly, their stepmother, had finally managed to coax the baby to sleep. Annie thought back to how when she had first met Dolly, she knew the woman as *Miss Dandridge*. Then she was *Dorothea*, and now, *Dolly*.

She smiled wanly at the girls, and Annie felt a twinge of worry for her new mother. "You must be awfully tired," she said, while offering her a drink from a jug of cider. "Father shouldn't have made you travel when the baby is still so young."

Dolly laughed. "Do you think I would let your father move to Leatherwood without me? I'm tired, but otherwise I'm perfectly well, and I'm strong as an ox. You just have to stop worrying about me," she said, with a smile that told Annie she was grateful for the concern.

"Well, I don't know why you couldn't convince Father to stay in Richmond," Betsy said, still not happy with the idea of being a frontier girl.

"I could no more keep your father in Richmond than you could keep Annie looking properly dressed," Dolly answered. "They both just go their own way."

"Annie looks wonderful," a new voice rang out. The three turned to see Patrick Henry walking toward them, with a spring in his step. He was a tall man but stoop-shouldered, and his balding head was hidden under a tie-back wig. He wore leather breeches and a stained leather vest that Annie knew was at least twenty years old.

"I think we'll camp here for the night," he said, looking around him. Annie's eyes followed his, and she could see that it was a good spot. The ground was level, with plenty of grass and water, and a good view of the trail behind them. It would be hard for a stranger to sneak up on them unawares.

"Are we almost there?" Betsy asked in a whining voice.

"Now, Betsy, you know I said the trip would take seven days if all went well. And we've been on the trail for only two. By my reckoning, that means five more days."

Betsy scowled. "Couldn't I have stayed with Aunt Anne?" she said.

The others exchanged glances, but Patrick Henry looked annoyed. "You are becoming tiresome, Betsy. I don't want to hear any more complaints."

Just then Annie remembered that she hadn't seen Neddy for a while. "Did Neddy ever find you?" she asked. "He saw a snake and wanted permission to shoot it."

Her father frowned. "I never saw him," he said. "How far back was that?"

Annie and Betsy looked at each other. The younger girl shrugged. "I wasn't paying much attention," she said.

Annie bit her lip. "He came riding hard out of a gully on the right. Maybe a mile back, but maybe not that far. Do you want me to go look for him?"

Patrick Henry shook his head. "He'll turn up. If he doesn't after a bit, I'll look for him," he said. He bent over and kissed his wife. "There's plenty of work to do here."

For the next half hour everyone was busy pulling the wagons into a circle, unhitching the teams of horses, gathering wood for the fire, and spreading out blankets for beds. Soon an aromatic stew bubbled in a big iron pot over the fire, and Annie felt her stomach grumble. Still, Neddy hadn't returned.

By looking at the sun, which hovered over the tree line to the west, Annie could tell it wasn't long until night fall. She worried about her father and Neddy. Finally, Annie grew so impatient with the wait that she went out on her own to search for her little brother. From one wagon to the next she looked, but there was no sight of him. Someone thought he had seen him get a musket, but no one could remember when that was. Annie wasn't worried that her brother had the gun. At nine, he was a good shot and had hunted often with his father. But that was at Scotchtown, where everything was familiar. Here, there were unfamiliar hills and gorges. A boy could easily get lost. Worse still, he could have been captured by Indians. The thought made Annie shiver and raised her determination to find him.

She retraced the trail that the wagons had traveled, hoping to catch sight of her father, until she had gone a mile or so. With the deepening shadows, it was hard to guess where the snake had been, so Annie looked for evidence of her brother. Finally, her sharp eyes saw where branches had been broken. She turned off the trail, thinking that this must have been the spot where Neddy had come charging out of the gully.

"Neddy," she called, while searching the brush for more clues. Her eye caught a glimpse of something white hanging from a tree branch. Scrambling off the path, her feet slipping on the loose gravel, and her long dress catching on the branches as she brushed by them, she reached and grabbed hold of a piece of cloth. It was a piece of white muslin, like the shirt that Neddy had been wearing.

Annie knew her brother had been this way, but was it recently or earlier in the afternoon? Should she go forward or back to the wagons? Glancing up at the pinkening sky, she knew that it would be dark very soon. If she didn't find Neddy, she would be alone with only wild animals to keep her company. That thought almost sent her scurrying up the path to the wagons.

"I can't leave him out here alone," she told herself. "I know Father is looking, but he didn't even know where to start. I don't want them to worry about me, but what can I do?" So she plunged on down the slope where she had found the piece of muslin. The dense brush caught at her skirt and scratched her arms. "Neddy!" she called again out loud.

By now evidence of Neddy was everywhere. Even Annie could see hoofprints in the wet soil near the creek at the bottom of the hill. How he had ever brought the horse into such deep brush, Annie couldn't tell.

All this time she had put fear out of her mind. She had to find her brother. But as the shadows deepened, Annie grew less confident, and tears welled up in her eyes.

In the dimming light, Annie strained to see in front of her. "Neddy, Neddy," she yelled. When she paused to listen, she heard the first sounds of the night. There was the hooting of an owl. Fireflies flickered, but her tears blurred their light. Had she been wrong to go after Neddy? It certainly seemed so now.

Wiping her eyes on the back of her hand, she pushed forward through the trees. Desperately she called out her brother's name and paused to listen. Was that a whimper? Again she called, this time more loudly.

At first it sounded like the cry of an injured animal, but as Annie listened, she heard her own name being called in response. Try as she might though, she couldn't see her brother.

"I can't see you," she yelled. "It's too dark. Yell louder."

The boy let go an awful cry that startled Annie with its closeness. She stumbled in the direction of the noise, fighting back tears of relief as she drew closer. Finally she saw him propped against a tree, his leg twisted awkwardly behind him. With a sob, she threw herself on her brother, letting her tears spill onto his head. That was enough to stop his noisy crying. He pulled away, wiping his hand across his shaggy hair. "Stop crying on me," he grumbled.

"All right," Annie agreed, wiping her eyes, but she

didn't take her arm away from her brother's shoulder, nor did he try to move it.

"Whatever happened to you?" she asked, when he had caught his breath and dried his own tears.

Sniffling noisily, Neddy said, "I went back to shoot that snake. Thought I had killed him, but when I rode Lightning up to take a look, the snake struck him on the shank. The horse reared back and threw me. I must have rolled down that hill. And then I tried to crawl to a safe place, but my leg is twisted. It hurts awful bad. I don't know where the horse went." His lip trembled as he thought about the wounded animal.

"Poor Neddy," Annie sympathized, patting him on the back, not wanting to think about the horse's fate.

The boy seemed to be watching the shadows. "You aren't alone, are you, Annie?"

She smiled ruefully. "I'm afraid I am. Father was out looking for you, but he didn't come back, and I couldn't bear to think of you out here alone, so I tried to find you myself. Problem is, night came too soon. I guess we'll have to spend it here together."

"No," Neddy screamed. "I can't be out here alone. Have you heard all the sounds?"

Annie hadn't been paying attention, but suddenly in the silence, she heard a distant howl.

"That's wolves," Neddy whispered. "There could be panthers, foxes, bears. We can't stay here alone."

"Well, we can't go back," she said matter-of-factly, though the thought of the wild beasts terrified her. "And there isn't any use in crying. That won't protect us. We're going to have to build a fire. A big one. Only problem is, I don't know how."

Neddy sat up straighter. "I have a flint. I can build a fire, but I can't get the wood. Not with this leg."

"Well, that's easy," Annie said. "I'll gather some wood. First, though, I'll have to move you." By pulling the boy up and letting him lean against her, they were able to shuffle off into the clearing. Annie's eyes had adjusted to the dark, and she was able to make out her brother's small shape, if she didn't wander too far. Being careful to keep him in sight, she filled her long skirt with twigs, which she carried back and forth to the site of the fire. Although there was no way of cutting larger pieces of wood, she found plenty of short pieces, which she dragged over.

Meanwhile, Neddy stacked the wood, placing twigs and dry leaves at the bottom. When he was satisfied, he pulled his flint out of his pocket and scraped it against a rock. It was tedious work, but finally a spark flashed in the dark, igniting the dry leaves and twigs. Soon the small pile of wood began burning. Annie gathered another skirtload, venturing a little further this time, since now she had the fire by which to see. Sparks spun their way into the night sky. Annie wondered if anyone could see them.

By the time she had gathered enough dry wood,

Neddy had slipped off into sleep. Annie huddled near him, musket at her side, and listened to the strange sounds that came from the dark forest. She knew her family would be worrying about them, but she also knew that it would be foolish for anyone to go out at night to find them. In the morning, she reassured herself; we'll be safe in the morning. As the fire crackled, she drifted off to sleep.

LEATHERWOOD

"WAKE UP," ANNIE URGED HER BROTHER. AROUND HER, the trees were shrouded by mist. Above them, the first hint of morning light brightened the sky.

"Do you hear that?" she whispered in his ear.

Neddy wiped the sleep from his eyes, which he opened reluctantly. "I hear you," he grumbled. "Let me sleep a little longer."

By now Annie was impatient to get back to her parents. She shook her brother until, grumbling, he sat up. "Listen," she demanded. "Don't you hear that noise?"

For a minute, the two sat in the shadows, straining to hear. "There it is again," Annie said. "It sounded like wood cracking."

"Probably a bear," he muttered.

"It isn't a bear. I think it's people," she said, brushing

the dirt from her skirt. She began throwing dirt on the embers of the fire until it was extinguished.

"If you don't get up," she said to her brother, who remained seated on the ground, "I'll leave you here."

"How am I supposed to walk?" he asked her. "Remember, my leg is sprained."

Annie felt like strangling her brother. It was bad enough that he had gotten lost and hurt, but now he was acting like a whiny baby. "If you get up, I'll help you up the hill," she managed to say, biting back the harsher words she felt like saying.

"I remember when you broke your wrist," Neddy said. "No one treated you mean. Why can't you be kind?"

"I'm trying," Annie said.

Annie took a deep breath but said nothing. She was thinking how miserable and ungrateful he was when she heard their names being called. "Annie . . . Neddy. . . ."

"We're down this gully," Annie screamed, hoping her voice could be heard.

She heard a shout and then another. Then her father's voice. "I'm coming down to get you," he yelled.

Annie and her brother waited as Patrick Henry scrambled down the steep slope. Finally, he stood before them, relief etched on his face.

"Thank God we found you," he said. "I searched until dark last night, and when I found Annie missing as well, I didn't know what to do. I couldn't leave Dolly and the baby. I couldn't sleep, thinking about you out here by yourselves." Then glaring at his son, he said, "Don't ever ride off alone like that. You could have caused great sadness."

Neddy hung his head, while Patrick Henry turned his attention to his daughter. "And you are old enough to know better." Annie frowned. She knew her father was right, though she didn't like hearing it.

He helped Neddy up the steep, wooded slope. There they met the rest of the search party that had left camp at dawn. Neddy rode in front of his father, while Annie rode behind John Fontaine. When they reached the camp, a cheer went up among all the people.

Later, when Annie was alone with Betsy, she learned that Dolly had been awake all night praying for their safe return.

After Neddy's adventure, the trip was uneventful. For five more days the train of wagons bumped and lurched its way along roads that got progressively worse until they were little more than worn ruts in the grass. They forded creeks and rivers and were glad for the large wheels of the Conestoga wagons that kept the wagon beds dry.

Annie and Betsy walked alongside the wagon when the bumping became more than they could bear. When their feet grew sore, they were forced to ride along some more.

What a sight they were! Annie marveled at the size

of her father's household. And she wondered at his desire to move so far out on the frontier. It seemed ridiculous to carry a fortepiano out into the wilderness, but that's what the Henrys were doing.

On the seventh day, the wagons climbed steadily up the hilly terrain. In the far distance, Annie could see a line of blue-gray mountains. It was the Blue Ridge, her father told her. The Henrys wouldn't be going past them but would settle in the foothills. This wild land thrilled Patrick Henry. Ever since the mountains had come into view, he had been excited. When they traveled through woods so dense that the sun never reached the forest floor, he pointed out various trees and animals.

More than once, Annie and Betsy were startled by a flock of wild turkeys that thundered up before the oncoming wagons. Neddy, confined to his wagon because of his leg, grumbled that he wasn't able to get a shot off at the inviting targets.

"How much longer?" Betsy asked for the hundredth time that day.

"Not more than a couple of hours," her father answered. "Isn't it beautiful?" Just then they heard the roar of a river, and looking over to the right saw the swirling waters of Leatherwood Creek. "We need only to follow the creek, and we'll be home," he said.

"Will it look like Scotchtown?" Betsy asked. "I don't want to share a room with anyone. Will I have my own?"

Patrick Henry sighed and looked at Annie, who had remained silent. "I trust, Daughter, that you will be content with whatever provision God has made for you."

Betsy blushed. "Couldn't God provide a nice big house like the Governor's Palace?" she whispered to Annie after her father had moved on.

"Shh," her sister cautioned her. "If you set your heart on a big house, you will surely be disappointed. Think of this as an adventure. Then you won't mind so much."

"That's easy for you to say," Betsy responded, her hand on her hip. "You had your chance to mix with society in Williamsburg. Now Father wants to bury us out here in the middle of nowhere. I swear I will die."

Annie giggled at her sister's words and her long face. "You might die at the hands of Indians, or maybe even a fever," she said dryly. "But I don't think you'll die for lack of luxury."

Before Betsy could respond, their father came riding back at a gallop. "It's just ahead," he said, hardly able to keep the grin from his face. "Take the wagons on about a mile," he told the driver, "and you'll see the house."

On down the line of wagons he went, giving the good news to his family that the long journey was finally at an end. Annie leaned forward with anticipation. Finally they would see the place where they would make their home for the next several years.

The horses strained to pull the wagons up the last hill,

and there at the top, Annie saw Leatherwood for the first time. She looked quickly at her sister, whose shocked expression told the whole story.

"Let's get down and go look it over," Annie urged. Betsy bit her quivering lip, trying hard not to cry. But tears, great big tears, slipped silently down her cheek.

"It's not so bad," Annie tried to reassure her. But Betsy would not be consoled, so the older girl hopped down from the wagon and went around to find Dolly. She found her stepmother near her wagon, holding little Dolly in one arm, with her other arm around her husband.

"Do you like it?" Annie heard him asking eagerly.

"It's good land," her stepmother answered. "Look at the timber. I've never seen anything like it. And we'll never want for game or fish. One can raise a family out here. I must admit that I am glad to be far from war. You've already sent two sons to fight. Is it selfish to want the rest of us to be safe?"

Without answering, he turned to his daughter whom he had just noticed. "Come, Annie. What do you think?"

She didn't want to hurt his feelings, but her face gave her away.

"I know the house is small," he said. "It isn't much more than a cabin, really. But we can add on to it and make it comfortable. There's plenty of good work to do, and we brought enough hands to do it."

Annie nodded doubtfully, but her father was so

excited that he didn't seem to notice her lack of enthusiasm. He rode off to give instructions, leaving Annie and Dolly watching in bemused silence.

Finally, Dolly said, "How is Betsy taking it?"

Annie smiled, "Not well, I'm afraid. Her heart is broken. She had hoped for a fine house like Monticello."

"Betsy has much to learn about the value of things. I think Leatherwood will be the place to learn it," Dolly said. "Now let's go see how bad it is."

Together, they strolled toward the house, calling to Betsy to join them.

"It's sturdy," Annie said finally, after the shock of seeing the tiny two-room house had passed. "Father was right to say it's sound. There aren't any holes in the roof, and the brick is tight."

"But it is so small," Betsy protested. "Where will we all sleep?"

"There's the loft," Dolly answered. "You and Annie will sleep up there. Father and I and the baby will take one of the rooms, and we'll put the table in the other."

"No," Betsy wailed. "What about parties? And won't we ever have visitors?"

Dolly was firm. "Betsy, you need to be content with what your father has provided for us. We can add on to it, but for now, the house is tight and secure. I know we'll be crowded, but we'll also be together. Your father has given Patsy and John Fontaine 2,000 acres down the creek.

They'll build their house over there. There are barns to build, quarters for the slaves, a place for Neddy. . . . We have too much to do to waste time worrying about parties."

While Betsy sniffled back her tears, Annie went through the house and out the backdoor. "There is a kitchen," she said. "Looks as though there is a smoke-house, also. She remembered the lessons she had learned in Williamsburg—character, not position, counts—and said, "It is not so bad."

Outside, there was all the commotion of a small village. Some slaves were unhitching the six mules from each wagon and leading them to a fenced pasture that Annie hadn't noticed before. Others were beginning to unload the family's furniture, carrying beds and tables and chairs into the two-room house.

Patrick Henry, striding out from the house, interrupted the work by calling to his foreman, "Nathan, moving this furniture can wait. I want two portholes built on each side of this house, big enough for a rifle to shoot through. Do you understand?"

The foreman nodded. He turned and spoke to several of the slaves nearest to him, who in turn nodded and went in search of tools.

Dolly, overhearing her husband's command, looked at him with surprise. "Portholes?" she asked. "Rifles? In our living room?"

"Now don't you worry, Dolly," he answered her soothingly. "It's only a precaution. You know there are Tory sympathizers and their Indian friends out here on the frontier. I'd be less than a good husband if I didn't try to protect you from them."

His wife nodded her head, but there was a look of sadness on her face, and Annie saw her hug her sleeping baby tightly to herself. Fearing that Betsy would throw another fit if she watched the slaves cut gunholes in the walls of the little house, Annie guided her sister away from the crowd. She found her older sister, Patsy, playing a guessing game with her son, Ben.

"Where will you live, Patsy?" Annie asked curiously. "Will you stay at the house with us?"

Her sister shook her head. "Father offered, but I want to be with John Fontaine," she answered softly. "I think they'll have a lean-to built by tomorrow, and then they'll set to work on a sturdy cabin. It won't be fancy, mind you, but it will be snug. I'll have the fortepiano, so I'll be content. Ever since John was injured in the army, I've wanted to be as far from war as I could get."

Glancing about, they both laughed. "It would be hard to get much farther away," Annie agreed.

Looking around at the dense woods that crept up one hill after another, Annie said, "There's no shortage of timber. But it seems as though there isn't much land cleared for farming. How will father ever make a go of it here?"

"I'd wager that he'll sell some wood," Patsy answered.

"John Fontaine told me that they'll girdle some of the trees this fall."

"What's that mean?" Betsy, who had been daydreaming nearby, interrupted.

"He says the men will cut all the bark away in a ring on each tree. Then next spring when the sap rises, it won't be able to, and eventually the trees will die. They'll harvest them, and we'll have plenty of lumber to build houses here."

"Just think of the exciting stories you'll have to tell," Annie coaxed her little sister. "Someday you'll be at a stuffy dinner party, where the only subject of conversation is how many rows of ruffles should decorate a lady's gown. You'll be able to spin a story of daring exploits in the wilderness. You'll shock them," she said with a grin on her face, enjoying the picture she was painting.

Betsy giggled in spite of herself.

Then Annie added with a broad smile, "Don't you know that Father's enemies would enjoy our present predicament? They'd love to think that Father was suffering in the wilderness. So we just have to prove them wrong. We'll show them what the Henrys are made of."

SQUATTERS

FALL OF 1779 CAME TO LEATHERWOOD IN A BURST OF color. Trees cast off their green clothes and put on yellow, orange, and outrageous shades of red until the nearby hills looked as if a huge patchwork quilt had been thrown over them. In the far distance, the mountains of the Blue Ridge seemed to stretch to the ends of the earth.

Annie felt surrounded by beauty more awesome than any she had imagined, and for the first time, she began appreciating what her father found so alluring about the frontier.

They were isolated. For days at a time, they saw no one outside the immediate family. They were hungry for news. So whenever travelers passed by, the Henrys urged them to stay and visit.

In November, a late-leaving group of settlers passed by on their way to Kentucky, bringing bad news of the war. The British had sent 3,000 troops by ship from New York to Savannah, hoping to capture the Georgia city. The British easily defeated the 800 Americans who defended it. Now the redcoats had an army in the South that promised to do much damage.

Annie despaired. Could it be that after more than four years of war the British would win? She did not worry for the Henrys' own personal safety. Savannah was a long way off, and their house was well-protected with the portholes, but she grieved for her country.

Though the colonies suffered, Leatherwood prospered. When she looked outside the house, Annie could see progress. The air was full of the rich smell of smoking hams. They wouldn't run short of meat that winter. Although they had arrived too late to plant crops, the ground was ready for spring planting. The Henrys had brought enough corn to see them through the winter.

The men kept busy building houses and clearing land, while the ladies tried to make their rude dwellings into homes. It fell to Annie to teach Betsy and Neddy. Neither liked studying, and more than once the older girl threw up her hands in frustration.

After one particularly hard day of teaching, Annie came upon her father, slumped over his desk, a letter in his hand. He didn't hear her at first, but when she saw him like that, she called out his name in a worried voice. Rousing himself, Patrick Henry tried to sit up and pretend that nothing was wrong, but his daughter saw the sweat on his forehead and the pallor underneath his tanned skin.

"Are you feeling sick?" she asked anxiously.

"I'm tired, and I think the fever may be coming on again," he said. "The air is so good here that I'm trusting not to be laid low by it, but all of the bustle of moving and building has sapped my strength and left me ripe for another bout."

"Then you must take to bed!" Annie urged him. She knew the fever, caused by malaria that he had contracted in the swampy city of Williamsburg, was often bad and had kept him in his bed for weeks at a time. "Maybe if you rest now, you can avoid the worst of it."

He gave her a weak smile. "There is wisdom in what you say, Daughter," he said. "But there is still much to be done before winter."

"It can be done without you," she said to him. "I'm sure Dolly would agree. Where is she?"

"She's gone to see Patsy for a bit. She'll be home soon," he said.

"Then you must go to bed now, and I'll have Martha come and tend to you."

Patrick Henry protested, but one look at his daughter's determined expression settled the question. When he rose to stand, she saw his legs sway, and he would have tumbled to the ground if she hadn't rushed to his side. He leaned heavily on her as they shuffled to the bed in the other room. No sooner had she settled him than his teeth began chattering and a drenching sweat broke out upon his brow.

With damp cloths Annie tried to bring down the fever. She paced nervously back and forth, listening anxiously for the sound of Dolly's return. Her father turned fitfully on his bed, groaning pitifully. Once, he sat upright, looked at his pacing daughter, and said grouchily, "You are giving me a headache. Can't you be calm?"

She bit her lip and forced herself to sit in the chair near the bed. Though she could make her body stay still, she couldn't keep her toes from tapping or her fingers from nearly rubbing the skin from her thumb. Just then, Dolly came into the little house.

Annie heard the door open and was out of her chair in an instant. Grabbing her stepmother's arm with relief, she said, "Father is ill with the fever. I've put him to bed, but I didn't know what else to do."

Dolly hurried into the sick room and saw that her husband had fallen asleep. Calmly, she straightened his bedcovers, rinsed the cloth and placed it back on his forehead, and closed several of the shutters so the room sank into dim shadows. Then turning to Annie she said, "You did everything that was necessary. All we need now is some of Martha's good potion. Would you go to her and have her bring some up to the house?"

Annie nodded and fetched Martha, the slave woman

who was gifted in medicine. She knew how to use herbs to heal almost any disease. Then Annie hung about the house, feeling that there was more she should do for her father. Finally, Dolly came to the door and said, "Why don't you take out one of the horses and go explore for a while? Your father should be fine. Hasn't God healed him each time? Doesn't Martha know how to treat him?"

Annie hesitated, unable to put away her worry.

"Come," said Dolly reassuringly. "Pray with me and then go. We will leave your father in the hands of his Father and Martha."

They prayed, but Annie still wouldn't go until Dolly said, "You aren't helping your father one bit by wearing a hole in the porch. Go!"

Reluctantly, Annie walked toward the stable, casting worried looks over her shoulder as she went. But when she reached the barn, her spirits lifted. She hadn't been riding for a long time. Dolly was right. She already felt better.

Joseph saddled her horse and led her out of the gated paddock. "Now don't you go too far," he scolded her. "No telling what kind of thing is prowling around out there."

But Annie, glancing up at the cloudless blue sky and feeling the crisp air on her cheeks, paid little heed to the warnings of the groom who seldom ventured out much beyond his stable.

She walked the horse slowly down the lane that led to the house, then turned him into one of the cleared fields. They trotted across, carefully avoiding stumps and rocks that littered the path. Once they were out of sight of the house, Annie felt her breath quicken. She loved exploring. She always had, and age had done nothing to dampen her enjoyment. In that way she was like her father, who never seemed able to settle in one place.

She had been riding for nearly an hour when she saw smoke wisping up over the next hollow. Cautiously, she urged the horse forward, hoping to see what was causing it. It could be travelers, she reasoned. But why would they be so far from the main trail? Could be Tories, those colonists who sided with the king. But why would they be on Henry land? It didn't make sense.

She stopped near a clump of trees and decided to go the rest of the way on foot. Sliding down from her saddle, she loosely tethered the horse to a tree branch. She crept forward, carefully avoiding sticks and leaves that would alert anyone to her presence. When she reached the top of the hillock, she cautiously peered over the crest and saw below a little shanty village made up of three makeshift houses clustered closely together. A little farther off was a fire with a huge kettle hanging over it.

Annie crouched behind a large outcropping of rock so that she was not visible from below. While she watched, three scruffy looking children, no older than Neddy, came tumbling out of one of the lean-tos. Behind them was a bearded man, dressed in buckskins, a musket in his hand. He bellowed at the children to keep quiet, then screamed back into the dark entrance of the shanty.

Out peered a bonnetless woman, who looked ancient to Annie. Her face was deeply lined. She had gaps in her mouth where her teeth should have been. A long pipe hung between her lips. She scowled at the loud-mouthed man before bustling toward the kettle. Grabbing a long, iron ladle, she began stirring whatever was in the pot, shooting sullen looks at the man. Meanwhile, he continued verbally abusing her until Annie's ears rang with ugly words she had never heard before.

Annie scooted back down the hill, eager to get away from the unpleasant scene. She mounted her horse and was ready to ride away when she thought again of the children. Could she just leave them there?

What else could she do? she asked herself. Those were surely their parents. Those children belonged with those adults. But maybe she could help them, she thought. The horse danced impatiently under her, eager to run in the crisp autumn air. Annie chewed her lip. What should she do?

Finally she made up her mind to tell John Fontaine. He would know who they were and what to do.

John was not at the Fontaine's little cabin. Patsy sat on a rocking chair on the front porch, a baby in her lap, and the two little ones playing contentedly in the dirt near by. Laundry hung from the line behind the house.

"Where are you going in such a hurry?" Patsy called out to her.

"I need to find John," Annie answered.

"I haven't seen him since breakfast," Patsy said. "He took a wagon and some shovels and went out that way. Said he was going to be putting up fences."

John wasn't more than a half mile away. She heard hammering before she found him supervising a crew that was fencing in a pasture for the cattle that the Henrys had brought with them from Scotchtown. When he heard Annie yelling and saw her galloping toward him, her dress flapping in the wind behind her, he threw down the piece of timber he was holding and ran toward her.

"Is it one of the children?" he asked, his face full of worry.

"Everyone is fine," Annie assured him, realizing suddenly how her sudden appearance must have scared him. "But I saw something that worried me." Annie sketched out the scene to her brother-in-law as quickly as she could.

After asking several questions, he frowned. "Squatters," he said.

"What?" Annie asked.

"They are squatters, I imagine. Folks told us there were some rough ones in these parts, but we hadn't seen them yet. They don't want to do honest labor. Sounds like they are making whisky, probably to sell to the Indians."

"Is it serious?" Annie wanted to know.

"Could be. Maybe they'll just leave if I tell them to. But that isn't likely. I think I'll go see Judge Lesker and have him supply a small posse to help me get them off the land. We don't want any trouble with them."

"What can I do?" Annie asked.

"You'll have to take me over to their camp," he answered. "Then I'll ride to the judge and see what he suggests. You get Patsy and take her up to the house. I don't want her alone until we know they're gone for good."

"How do we know they are the only ones?"

"I expect they aren't. That's one reason I want Judge Lesker and some help. Usually these squatters will set up different camps. If one is found, they all move on to another."

John barked out instructions to the crew, then mounted his horse and they were on their way. Annie didn't have any trouble finding the camp again.

"Get Patsy and take her up to your father's," John commanded. "It probably isn't necessary, but I'll feel better knowing she isn't alone. I'm going to get the judge. No telling when I'll be back."

At Patsy's, Annie helped her sister pack up some clothes and ready the babies. Together they hitched up a wagon, tied Annie's tired horse to the back, and drove over to the larger house. For once she was glad for her father's foresight in putting in the portholes.

Only when she came in view of the house did she remember her father's relapse. In all the confusion, she had put it out of her mind. Turning to her older sister, she said, "Father is in bed again. He looks bad, but we caught it early this time, and Dolly says not to worry. I wanted to tell you, though, so you wouldn't be taken by surprise."

The color drained from Patsy's face as she listened calmly to her younger sister. Her eyes stared into the distance, only her trembling lip revealed her worry.

All of Annie's own fears returned. Yet she knew that her worrying wasn't going to help her father. "I believe God will preserve him a little longer," Annie whispered, as her sister buried her face in her nursing baby's hair. "You will have to trust Him for that."

Of course there was confusion when the sisters reached home. Now instead of six, there were ten people in the house, one of whom was very sick.

Neddy whined because he was left at home with the girls. Betsy cried because she didn't like living in the wilderness. Though Dolly tried to bring order to the confusion, Annie could see she was on the verge of tears herself.

"Betsy," she said, "You take care of the baby and let Dolly go back to Father." When Betsy began to protest,

Annie interrupted. "I'm going to take Benjamin and go for a walk with Neddy."

"But you can't leave," Patsy said.

"We won't go out of sight of the house," Annie promised. "The boys will climb the walls if we stay."

Outside, the sky had darkened. Thick thunderheads billowed above, and the leaves of the nearby trees flashed silver in the wind.

"Doesn't it smell like rain?" Annie asked, trying to distract the boys while hoping to catch a glimpse of John Fontaine.

"If it rains they'll come home, won't they?" Neddy asked.

"I think they'll probably stay until the job is done," Annie answered.

Benjamin squealed as the first raindrop plopped on his face. "Rain rain," he chanted. The drops fell one by one at first, but then the sky opened and the torrent poured down.

"Run to the house," Annie shouted, scooping up Benjamin in her arms.

They pushed through the door, laughing and letting the water drip off their clothes onto the floor. Patsy looked up. "Don't tell me it's raining," she moaned, putting down her sewing and hurrying to the window to look out. "Look at it come down. Surely they'll come home and not stay out in the rain."

But John did not come home that night or the next day, even though the rain continued. To the ten anxious souls crowded into the small house, the rain seemed to go on forever. At the first sign of a break in the weather, Annie announced that she was going to the stable.

"Is it safe?" Dolly asked.

"Of course it is," Annie replied. "We haven't seen or heard a sound for days. I cannot stay inside any longer."

"Then go if you must," Dolly said in a weary voice. "But take the musket with you. John left it loaded."

Annie carried the heavy gun outside with her. The air was crisp and frosty, but bundled up in her cloak, she was warm. Crossing through the muddy yard, she was glad for the galoshes on her feet.

Once she reached the stable, she didn't want to stay there. She asked Joseph to saddle her horse, feeling confident because of the musket that she carried. Off she rode, letting the horse determine the direction in which they went. She had intended to stay near the house, but gradually they rode further afield until the smoke from the chimney was no longer visible.

Now curiosity took over. Annie led the horse on the path toward the squatters' camp, sure that John had chased them away by now. She rode the horse boldly up the hillock, not bothering to hide her presence. When she reached the top, it was just as she had thought. No fire burned, and there was no sign of any occupants.

She led the horse down the rocky trail toward the camp, keeping her hand on the musket for security. Once at the bottom, she tethered the horse and explored. The little dirt-floored shacks were empty of everything except a few pieces of chipped pottery. Annie didn't know if they had ever held furniture, but whatever had been there was now gone.

She was glad to leave the pathetic little camp. Riding on, she heard the sound of horses and the creaking of wagon wheels. Riding on a bit farther, she saw a bedraggled band of squatters walking slowly down the trail, two men pulling a cart loaded with household items behind them.

Watching the procession, muskets at their sides, were John Fontaine and a band of ten mounted men. He turned when he heard the sound of Annie's horse advancing from behind him. When he saw her, his face darkened with anger. He broke off from the watching group and rode toward her, a grim expression on his face.

Annie tried to smile and explain, but he interrupted. "Didn't I tell you to stay inside?" he barked.

"Yes, but . . ."

"I don't want to hear any 'yes buts,'" he said bluntly. "You don't know what kind of danger you might have walked into."

"Oh, but John, you don't know how hard it was to

wait. Inside with all those people, and the rain. . . ." she said, hoping he would soften.

"Annie," he said sternly. "It hasn't been easy being outside in the rain, either. But we had a duty, and we did it. You also had a duty, which you chose not to do. You cannot be driven by how you feel. . . . You must learn to do what's right, even when it costs you comfort or tries your patience."

The straggling trail of squatters had passed from sight, with the mounted men behind them. John watched until the horsemen too were out of sight. Then sighing, he said to his sister-in-law, "Come, let us go home."

Annie sighed. She didn't like being reprimanded by John. It made her feel like a little child once again. As they rode along in silence, she thought about his criticism. Maybe he was right. Maybe she had acted impulsively, doing what she felt like. She would need to think about it more. She glanced sideways at her brother-in-law. His wet coat hung heavily and water dripped from his tricorner hat. He slouched in his saddle, his eyes closed as if he were asleep.

For several minutes longer they rode along without speaking. It was John who broke the silence. "Aren't you curious about what happened?" he asked.

"Of course I am, but I thought you were too weary to answer."

"We found five camps. That's what took so long. They

were hidden in hollows that were near impossible to find. There were a few women and children, poor things, but mostly it was ragged men. I wouldn't be surprised if some weren't deserters from General Washington's army."

"Deserters?" Annie asked.

"Men who couldn't take the long winters in the North without any food or proper boots. General Washington's army lives on air, don't you know?"

That brought a small smile to his quiet face.

"Was there fighting?" Annie asked.

"None worth speaking about," he said. "Several of the men were so drunk they couldn't even put their trousers on straight. None of them could shoot a gun, not in the condition they were in."

"Where will they go to?"

"I don't know. Judge Lesker told them that if they were found in Henry County, they'd be arrested as deserters, and that seemed to scare them. He's escorting them to the North Carolina border. I don't think they'll come back, not to these parts anyway."

By now they had reached the house. "You go on in," Annie said. "I've got some thinking to do."

A WILD RIDE

WHEN WINTER CAME TO LEATHERWOOD, THE SNOW made travel extremely difficult. Mail already took weeks to reach them, and the snow only made it slower. In January, 1780, Dolly gave birth to another daughter. They named her Sarah Butler, which Annie liked because her mother's name had been Sarah. Now the house was more crowded than ever.

In February, Patrick Henry received notice that he had been elected to the Virginia legislature by his neighbors in Henry County. The notice came to him so late that the session had already started. When he received it, he and Annie were sitting in the barn where he was oiling his saddle.

"It's seven days ride in the best of weather," he told Annie, glancing up from the letter he had just received. "I can't make it in less than ten in these conditions.

Besides, Dolly would hate to have me go so soon after the baby's birth."

"Won't they miss you, though?" Annie asked. She pulled her long cloak more tightly around her neck, feeling the sharp wind as it blew through the drafty barn.

"They may miss me, though Governor Jefferson might welcome my absence. In any case, the letter is so late in arriving that I couldn't get there in time. I will write a letter declining to attend this session. Perhaps in May I'll go."

Annie groaned inwardly. The whole family had thought that moving to Leatherwood would bring an end to Patrick Henry's frequent absences from home. But it seemed as though his neighbors thought too highly of him to keep him out of the legislature.

"How will you tell Dolly?" Annie asked him gently, knowing that her stepmother wouldn't like being left with two small babies on the frontier.

Her father rubbed his jaw and gave his silk cap an absentminded tug. "Dolly knew when she married me that I had a duty to Virginia," he said. "She won't be happy, but she will accept it as my calling from God."

"I almost wish that I were going," Annie confessed. "I'm feeling a bit crowded in this little house with all these people. I need some kind of work to do, I think, because I fritter away my time in so many unproductive pursuits."

Patrick Henry studied his daughter's serious face. "I

thought you were teaching Neddy and Betsy," he reminded her. "That is important work."

"Indeed it is," Annie answered. "But they are such poor students. Betsy would rather daydream about missed parties in Richmond, and I can't force her to study. She just looks at me and shrugs. And Neddy. He is even worse. His Latin is poor, and my Greek is worse. Between the two of us, we scrape through the lessons. But, Father, surely you see that I am not equipped like Mr. Dabney to teach."

He smiled. "Neddy doesn't take much to learning, that I know," he answered kindly. "And Betsy is so pretty, she probably won't have to know more than she does right now. Some young man will want to marry her, not for her book learning and conversation, but for her good temper and pleasant company. Do the best you can, my dear. Neither I nor God would ask anything else."

Annie listened with resignation. She knew her father's words were true. She knew enough to teach her sister and brother all that they might need to know. Neddy would probably be a frontiersman all his days. The reading and ciphering he already could do put him ahead of many of the men of that type. And he was right about Betsy, also. She was pretty and self-confident, and when she wasn't complaining, she did have a sweet, gentle spirit. Then why did his words make Annie so sad?

She rose from the hay where she had been sitting. "I must go and do something," she said in response to his worried look. "Every part of me wants to scream for being cooped up so long. I wish I could just go run like I did when I was a child. I almost regret getting older. I'm trying," she confessed, "but I don't seem suited for those womanly tasks."

Her father reached out and patted her shoulder. "You'll find your calling, and God will equip you for it," he said. "Go inside and see if you can't relieve Dolly of some of her burdens. You'll see. Helping her will take your mind off your own troubles."

Annie pulled her cloak more tightly around her shoulders and headed out into the bitter winter cold. The wind, whipping through the opening between the house and the barn, caught Annie in the face, making her gasp for breath. Underfoot, the frozen ground crunched as she crossed the yard. She was paying so much attention to her efforts to keep her skirts off the ground that she didn't spot a patch of ice. When her foot slipped out beneath her, she swung her arms wildly, trying to maintain her balance, and landing on her seat on the ice. Her cloak flew open, and the bitter wind found its way inside her woolen dress. As she stood up, Neddy appeared from behind the house.

"Ha ha." he laughed, pointing at Annie. "I saw that."

"Oh be quiet," she muttered as she stumbled up the stairs.

The wind followed her into the little house, until she slammed the door on it. Inside, Betsy and Dolly stitched and talked in front of the fireplace, while the children either slept or played nearby.

"Come in and get warm," Dolly said, looking up and seeing her wild-haired stepdaughter standing near the door. "You must be freezing."

"What I'd like to do," Annie blurted out, "is go visit Patsy. She's probably feeling housebound, and if I took a wagon I could be there in a half hour or so."

"But it is too cold," Dolly objected. "You'll get sick."

"I'll put on extra clothes," Annie promised. "And we can heat some bricks to put by my feet. There's a heavy bearskin rug . . . . Why I'll be toastier on the wagon than you are here by the fire."

Dolly sighed. "I know you're feeling housebound, dear," she said sympathetically. "You may go, but you bundle up tightly."

At that moment, Annie loved her stepmother more than ever, and tears welled up in her eyes. She always seemed to understand what her stepdaughter was feeling, even when Annie couldn't put it into words. She smiled gratefully at the older woman, who blew her a kiss across the room.

Neddy barged in the door behind her. "Can I come too?" he begged. Annie groaned inwardly, but she didn't need to worry. Dolly shook her head.

"Shut the door and take off your wet clothes, young man. We'll let your sister go off on her own for a little bit."

By the time Annie was settled on the wagon, the wind had died down, but the air was still frigid, and her cheeks burned with the cold. Under the bearskin, however, she was toasty warm. She urged the horses along the frozen trail, up and down the small hills, until the Henry house was out of sight behind her.

There was a high point between the two houses. When Annie reached it, she stopped the wagon and listened. Out on the frontier it was quiet. Except for the creaking of a branch in the wind, there was no sound at all. No sound of slaves working in the fields. No sound of hammering or sawing. No sound of horses. No laughing or talking or running or crying. It was completely silent, and Annie imagined for a minute that she was the only person alive.

She shivered at the thought. Is that what she wanted—to be alone? Rousing herself from her daydream, she clucked to the horses, urging them on toward Patsy's. Annie was about halfway there when she came to a long stretch of road that went through dense forest. They had cleared a trail only wide enough for a wagon to pass. On a bright sunny day when the leaves were in full leaf, the canopy was so dense that little light reached the forest floor. Even on a winter day when the trees were bare, the path was plunged in shadows.

She urged on the horses. Suddenly, and without warning, they stopped. Though Annie slapped the reins and clucked until her mouth was dry, the two horses would not budge. "Now what is wrong?" she muttered into the frosty air as the horses nervously pawed the ground. She stood up on the board seat and looked around.

As she stood there, trying to see what had set the horses off, one of them reared up and threw himself against his harness. The wagon lurched forward, and Annie was thrown to the ground.

She landed with a thud on the bearskin that had slipped off her lap when she stood. "Fool horses," she muttered as she rubbed her hip where she had hit the ground. About fifty feet ahead, the horses stopped. They pawed the ground and acted so skittish that she feared they might run away.

Gathering up the bearskin, she crept forward, not wanting to scare them off. It was then that she saw what had frightened them—two wolves lurking behind the trees about twenty yards from the wagon. Their bony bodies looked half-starved, but that only made them appear more dangerous. Annie quickened her pace. Had they seen her? she wondered.

The closer she crept to the wagon, the closer she drew to the wolves. They were walking in a circle, keeping Annie and the wagon in the center. The girl scanned the trees, but she did not see any others. Didn't they always travel in packs? By now the two horses were going crazy, scraping the ground, rearing and tossing their heads.

When Annie was about five yards away, she began to run. At the same moment the wolves rushed forward. She threw herself on the back of the wagon, her legs tangling in the long skirt of her dress, just as the horses took off running. Clinging to the flat bed of the careening wagon, Annie inched forward until she had reached the seat.

The two snarling and growling wolves snapped at the wooden wheels as the horses gathered speed. They were joined by five more that Annie hadn't seen before. The pack raced along, seeming to keep pace with the horses. Clinging desperately to her seat, she looked at the reins hanging just out of reach. If she couldn't grab them, the horses would run the out-of-control wagon into a tree.

Annie clutched the seat as the wagon veered off the track and almost hit a tree. "If I don't grab the reins we'll surely crash, and then I'll die," she moaned, closing her eyes as if that would keep her from harm. "Lord, help me," she prayed.

The words had barely left her lips when she opened her eyes and saw the reins hanging just beyond her reach. She inched forward on the seat, turning slightly so her right arm was closer to the reins, while she continued clutching with her left. "Now!" she said to herself as she reached and caught the leather straps in her hand. The smooth leather cut into her hand as the horses strained against the reins, but Annie ignored the pain and wrapped the straps around her palm so she couldn't let go. She tried to calm the horses without slowing them, but it was a hopeless task with the wolves snapping at their heels.

There was a thump. Annie looked behind her and saw the crumpled body of a wolf that had somehow been crushed by the wagon. The other wolves slowed and circled back. She turned away, not wanting to see them tear into its still-warm flesh.

On they ran through the last of the forest trail, going much faster than was safe on that wild stretch of road. Finally, they reached the open trail again, then up a rise, and Patsy's cabin came into view. Aromatic smoke drifted from the cabin's stone chimney. The horses, sensing safety, finally heeded Annie's direction and allowed themselves to be brought under control.

Annie led the wagon around to the barn, ignoring the cold. When she stumbled across the threshold of the snug little cabin, Patsy could see immediately that something had happened. She put down the baby and poured a cup of hot herb tea, which she urged on her sister.

Annie couldn't keep her teeth from chattering. Everytime she tried to talk, the words got lost in sobs. Finally Patsy shushed her. "Just drink the tea and warm yourself," her sister urged. "There will be time for words later."

A GREAT WIND

SPRING BROUGHT MORE BAD NEWS TO THE COLONISTS. The victory at Savannah gave London's generals confidence to try an attack against Charleston, South Carolina. In February, 10,000 British soldiers attacked Charleston. About 5,000 Americans were waiting for them, but only half were professional soldiers. The rest were militiamen who had come from their farms to defend Charleston and all of South Carolina. Reports from the continuing battle were vague, but the British seemed to have the upper hand. The Henrys at Leatherwood, like patriots everywhere, prayed for good news.

Annie was becoming impatient. Even watching spring come to Leatherwood couldn't cheer her. Everywhere there were signs of new life. Leaf buds swelled on the trees, and tender grass sprang up from barren ground.

It was too soon, of course, to put away winter clothes

and blankets. In March there could still be a month of cold weather ahead. One day while she was walking, Annie noticed that not all of Leatherwood's trees had come to life. Some stood naked against the blue sky, not a bud on their barren branches.

"Father, why do some of the trees look as though they are dying?" she asked one night at supper. "There is a large grove of hardwoods without a leaf."

"Don't you remember? Those are the trees that we girdled last autumn," he told her. "We cut a ring through the bark so the sap can't run. They're dying, and it will make it easier for us to cut them down next year."

"You'll wait a whole year?" she asked.

"It takes a long time to kill a tree," he replied. "But without a canopy of leaves, the sun will finally reach the ground and warm the soil so we can plant corn around them."

Neddy interrupted. "Won't it be hard to plow, with all the trees in the way?"

"We won't harvest as much, but we will get a crop. Next year, when the trees are completely dead, we will clear them out."

"But what about all the other trees?" Neddy asked, since only one grove had been girdled.

"You'll have to wait and see," his father replied.

Several days later, Annie woke to the sounds of branches scraping against the roof. The wind moaned as it chased through the cracks under the doors. Though it was still dark outside, she heard her father's voice and saw light through the door of the loft.

Betsy muttered in a voice thick with sleep, but Annie ignored her, knowing that her sister would drift off if left alone. The older girl shivered in the cold loft. She darted from the warmth of her bed and retrieved her dress and woolen stockings, which she put on as quickly as she could before scurrying down the ladder.

Someone had already put fresh logs on the fire, and voices from her parents' room let her know that both Dolly and her father were awake. Annie poured herself a cup of herb tea, grabbed a biscuit, and had breakfast in front of the fire while she waited for them to come out. Something was going on, and Annie wanted to know what it was. Maybe they had heard from her brothers at the war.

Soon her father opened the door. When he saw his daughter sitting in front of the fire, a smile split his face. "I'm not surprised to see you up," he said.

"I heard voices, and since it is still dark outside, I thought I would see what was going on," she said.

"I could tell you to go back to bed," her father said smiling. Just then Dolly walked out of the room carrying baby Sarah in her arms. She looked sleepy, and Annie saw that her stepmother hadn't bothered to dress. She had pulled a warm dressing gown over her nightgown, and her hair was still mussed from sleep.

"Did he wake you as well?" Dolly asked with a wan smile. "I told him to whisper, but you know your father."

Annie smiled. "You look like you didn't get much sleep. Was the baby fussy?" she asked sympathetically.

"I don't know what it is," Dolly admitted with a worried frown. "She fussed most of the night, and just when she had fallen to sleep and I had dozed off, your father heard the wind."

"But Father," Annie said, "what's so special about the wind?"

"We're clearing acres today," he said with a gleeful expression.

He poured himself a glass of cider and munched on several biscuits left over from the night before. "I promised John Fontaine that I would be over at first light if there promised to be a good wind today. I must be hurrying," he added, peeking out the window.

A look of confusion crossed Annie's face. "I don't understand," she said.

"If you want to come with me," he told her, "then you will see why I'm so excited by the wind. If you'd rather stay here, I'll tell you about it later."

It took Annie about five seconds to decide that she'd rather be outside with her father than in the little house with a fretful baby, a tired mother, her cranky sister, and a toddler who would need minding.

Annie rose to find her cloak and muff.

"Wear thick boots," her father said. "And make sure you're plenty warm. We'll be gone all day."

With all her layers of clothes, Annie felt as she imagined a bear would feel in his winter fur. She waddled out to the waiting wagon where Neddy, similarly bundled, bounced eagerly on a bale of hay. "Isn't this grand?" he said excitedly, tying a red knit scarf tightly around his neck.

Annie smiled at her brother. Looking in the back of the wagon, she found many axes. Her father strode forth from the house, dressed like a woodsman, anticipation on his face.

They set off slowly for the Fontaine cabin, the wagon slogging through the muddy trail. At the far edge of the woods that separated the two houses, Patrick Henry stopped the wagon. Before long, John arrived with a wagonload of slaves. Annie watched her father and John talking, their conversation punctuated by gestures as they pointed at various trees.

Annie huddled under a bearskin. The crew of men walked toward a stand of trees to her right. Soon, the forest echoed with the sound of metal against wood, as the men cut triangle-shaped notches into the trees. Wood chips flew until the air was thick with dust.

For several hours the men labored, sweat pouring down their faces despite the cold. Annie's ears rang with the noise, and she started wishing she hadn't come. Then suddenly the noise stopped. The sweating men drifted out toward the trail, sawdust stuck to their wet clothes and skin.

They quenched their thirst with dippers of water from the barrel and mopped their foreheads with the back of their sleeves. She watched them and didn't notice that one man had stayed in the woods. The sound of his ax rang out, startling her. When she turned, she saw a powerfully built man standing at the base of a tree that towered above all the others. He looked small against the trunk of the huge tree, and his ax seemed a tiny tool to take on the mighty trunk.

The wind roared, forcing Annie to pull the bearskin more tightly around herself. "Boom," went the sound of the ax against wood. On the lumberman labored, each stroke of the ax seeming as strong and steady as the first blow he had landed. Finally, he had cut a notch about halfway through the trunk. He looked up at the tree, which swayed in the wind, and took one more swing before running out of the forest faster than Annie had ever seen a man run.

She was more puzzled than before. They had cut notches out of nearly one hundred trees, as near as she could tell. But not one had come down. How were they supposed to clear a field like this?

Just then her father strode around the wagon. "Are

you ready, Daughter?" he asked, a broad grin stretching across his face.

"Ready for what?" she replied. "I must not understand tree clearing, because it seems to me you haven't cleared a one."

"Patience," he answered with a sly grin. "Before this day is done, this whole stand will be clear. Remember, things often don't seem as they are."

Her father walked away from the wagon, clearly enjoying his mystery. Annie smiled and let him have his fun. The trees moaned in the wind, and overhead a flock of blackbirds squawked noisily.

It was hard to wait, especially when she didn't know what she was waiting for. The men huddled around, telling each other stories and laughing as they ate cornbread and drank cider, not at all minding the rest from their work.

Out of the corner of her eye, Annie caught a glimpse of red darting behind a tree. When she turned to get a better look, it was gone. Thinking it was a cardinal, she stared into the woods hoping to see it again.

The next time she saw it, she realized it was too big to be a bird. Suddenly Annie remembered Neddy. Hadn't he been wearing a red scarf? She tried to remember. Climbing down from the wagon, she ran a few feet into the woods. "Neddy," she called out.

There was no answer, so Annie ran in a little farther

and called his name a little louder. Then she saw the flash of red again. "Neddy!" she screamed.

"Help me," he called to her.

Annie felt her heart beat faster. Now what trouble was he in? She found him squatting on the ground. "What are you doing?" she asked.

"I found this perfect skeleton," he answered. "If I try to pick it up, it will break apart."

"Oh, Neddy," Annie said a little crossly. "What do we need with a dirty old possum skeleton, anyway?"

"Come on," he whined. "It will be part of my collection. I can draw it and study it. Please?"

"Well, what do you want me to do?" she asked.

"Put it in your skirts," he said, as though that were the most obvious thing in the world.

Annie looked with a mixture of fondness and exasperation at her little brother. "All right," she answered. "But I'm not touching it. If you want the dirty old thing, you pick it up yourself."

The boy carefully lifted the small bundle of bones and set it on Annie's skirt, where she cradled it in the folds. "Now, we better leave these woods," she said. "The men are waiting for something."

The two walked slowly toward the trail, Annie being careful not to jiggle the bones that her brother had gone to such lengths to attain. Just then, there was an enormous gust of wind, followed closely by the loud cracking of wood. The girl looked up and saw above her the huge tree trembling and shaking. Its enormous trunk swayed violently as the wind blew against it. There were more sounds of wood cracking, and Annie understood instantly the danger that she and Neddy were in.

"Run!" she screamed at her brother, dropping her skirts and running as fast as she could.

He bent over as if to retrieve the skeleton that she had just dropped, but Annie screamed again. "Don't bother with it. Just run!" Even as she spoke, the tree swayed further as its trunk, where it had been notched, began to give way.

Annie and her brother stumbled out of the woods just as the tree was torn from its stump and crashed into the tree next to it. That tree, which had also been notched, trembled and shook. Unable to stand up to the weight of the huge tree that leaned upon it, that tree also snapped, falling on the tree next to it. One after another the trees fell, the ground shaking as their heavy trunks crashed to the forest floor. When Patrick Henry saw his children dash out only a moment before the first tree fell, he ran to them.

By the time he reached them, they were at the wagon, where Annie hugged the frightened boy while she fought off tears of her own. How close they had come to death, she thought.

She didn't know whether to laugh or cry. Laugh,

because she was saved. Cry, because she had come too close to death.

Patrick Henry met them with stunned silence. When he could finally speak, he said to Annie sharply, "What were you doing in there?"

Her eyes welled with tears, but before she could answer, Neddy said, "She saved my life, Father. Don't be angry."

From behind them came the din of splitting wood as more trees thudded to the forest floor. But the drama of the trees seemed like nothing compared to the drama of life and death in which they had almost been a part.

Clutching his children tightly to himself, Patrick Henry bowed his head and prayed.

By the end of the day, not a single tree stood in what had been a dense stand of forest. The ground was littered with their heavy trunks, which lay in piles where they had fallen. It would take days for the men to drag them away, and still more days for the stumps to be burned and hauled away. Finally, the field would be ready for planting.

There would be time in the future to think of those tasks. Patrick Henry looked out over his land with a contented sigh. "This is good land," he told his children. "We serve a most gracious God. How blessed we are!"

A HORRIBLE DISCOVERY

IN MAY, 1780, THE NEWS FROM THE WAR WAS WORSE. The American soldiers in Charleston had surrendered, and the British were in a position to control all of South Carolina. From there they could threaten North Carolina and even Virginia. "Why is this happening?" Annie cried. "I thought we were going to win the war. I never expected that we would lose."

"Patience, Annie," Dolly answered. "Doesn't your father always say that there is much that goes on beyond our sight—and even beyond our understanding. Surely you have learned to trust the Lord."

"Feebly, I guess," came Annie's reply. "It is always easier to trust when things are going well."

"Ah, yes," Dolly said smiling. "But faith is believing in things not seen, in things yet hoped for."

Annie thought about Dolly's words the next morning

as she lay in bed listening to the blue jays yammering outside. Pulling her pillow over her ears, she tried to block out the noise, but it only grew worse as the gray squirrels added their chatter to the confusion.

The girl threw off her pillow, which hit Betsy on the ear.

"Annie," the younger sister complained. "Why did you throw your pillow at me?"

"Just listen to those birds," Annie complained. "How can you sleep so soundly?"

Betsy rolled over in the bed the girls shared. "You're just out of sorts because Father has gone to the assembly," Betsy said. "Now go back to sleep and stop bothering me. I'm tired."

Annie glared at her sister's back. Betsy always slept like a log, but Annie couldn't sleep when she was troubled. "I'm to be content in all things," she muttered, wishing it were easy to put those words into practice. "If only I knew what my future would bring. How can I be content buried out here on the frontier where there is no one my age and no prospects of marriage? Will I live with my father and all his new children all the days of my life?"

She sighed deeply as she rose from her bed. The face that greeted her in the looking glass made her scowl. Annie's cheeks were freckled from the sun because she often forgot to wear her bonnet. Her curly brown hair refused to be tamed, so Annie had taken to wearing it pulled back in a knot at her neck. She pinned on her white lace cap, tucking the stubborn curls underneath.

"Good morning," her stepmother said, looking up fondly as she came into the room. "You look fresh this morning."

"I don't feel fresh," Annie confessed grumpily. "I feel uglier than sin, and my mood matches."

"Is it because your father has gone?" Dolly asked.

"No . . . though I wish he were done with politics. Just like I wish the war were over."

"May I ask you a question?" Annie blurted, feeling shy all of a sudden.

"Of course, what is it?"

"Do you think . . . um," Annie hesitated and then started again. "Is it possible? . . . Do you think I'll ever get married?"

"You're not yet seventeen," Dolly answered. "You'll have time."

"But will I ever meet someone and fall in love?" she asked.

"Poor dear," Dolly answered, rising from her chair and putting her arms around Annie. "If God has called you to marriage, then he'll provide a godly man to be your husband. But my Annie has never found it easy to wait, have you?" Holding Annie at arm's length she considered, "Why don't you go up and visit Clara Lesker? It'll do you good to see a friend."

It was a lovely May day. As the horse ran, Annie found her dark thoughts being replaced by a sense of well-being. She breathed deeply of the rich smell of damp soil and fragrant wildflowers. She saw rhododendron thickets so dense that a man could not cross them. Bees and butterflies hovered near their showy flowers.

Judge Lesker and his wife, Clara, lived in a house on a nearby parcel of land close to Martinsville, about two miles away. Mrs. Lesker was a young woman who had taught school in Williamsburg before moving to the frontier with her husband, a young lawyer. After several years he had become a county judge, riding circuit over Henry County, hearing cases in even the most remote locations. Several times Annie had visited with her, and the two enjoyed remembering life in Williamsburg.

The Leskers lived in a large frame house made of lumber planed in the lumber mill at Danville. Annie knew the house had been costly because the lumber had to be brought all that way over rough, hilly roads. But that was one of the reasons the girl liked to visit. It reminded her of Scotchtown; it was roomy and filled with pretty things from back East. And Mrs. Lesker was so happy in her marriage. "If only I could have her good fortune," Annie said to herself as she dismounted.

Annie tied the horse up at the fence and walked to the front door. The house seemed strangely quiet. She hoped the Leskers hadn't gone away. After knocking softly and getting no response, she examined the windows. They weren't shuttered. She looked up and saw that there was no smoke coming from the chimney. That was strange. People never let their fires go out because it was difficult to start another.

The door was not locked, and it pushed open easily. Feeling just a little skittish, Annie peeked into the hall, calling out softly, "Mrs. Lesker?"

There was no response. Annie looked around nervously. "Don't be foolish," she told herself. "You are acting jumpy like an old woman. Why, the Leskers probably went away overnight and just forgot to lock up."

Pushing the door open all the way, Annie forced herself to enter the quiet house. She called out again, wishing that her voice did not sound so shaky. When there was no response, she began to feel better. Surely they had just gone away. "I guess I'll lock the shutters for them," she said to herself. "That way no squatters will be coming into the house while they are gone."

The girl closed the shutters in the front parlor and the study, wishing there was at least a fire in the fireplace to brighten up the dark rooms. She crossed over the hallway to the front bedroom and pulled its shutters closed, hurrying out to the hallway, which was well-lit by the still-opened door.

There was one more room before Annie could get back on her horse and head to Leatherwood. She pushed open the door of a gloomy bedroom, which was shaded by a large bush growing outside the window.

Annie sniffed. What was that smell? she wondered, putting a handkerchief over her nose. She hurried to the window and pulled the shutter closed, wanting only to get out of the house as quickly as she could. As she began locking the shutter, she heard a quick intake of breath coming from the bed.

Annie spun around. There, huddled in the corner of the bed, was Mrs. Lesker, rocking back and forth, clutching a pillow between her arms. Her wild black eyes stared forth from her pale, tear-streaked face.

Without thought of danger, Annie rushed forward and threw her arms around the frightened woman. Stroking the woman's tangled hair, Annie said, "What is wrong? What has happened?"

Mrs. Lesker moaned, and the tears streamed down her face.

"Let me get you a drink," Annie whispered. She let go of Mrs. Lesker, but as she did so, the women began trembling. Annie was crossing the room to fetch the water from the washstand when the woman let out a shriek, nearly scaring the girl to death. "Whatever is the matter?" she demanded—and stumbled over Mr. Lesker, who lay in a crumpled heap upon the floor.

Annie forgot the water. She bent down, her face close to his, listening for a breath. There was nothing. Gently, she rolled the lifeless man onto his back. A crimson stain spread across the front of his shirt near a ragged, powder-stained hole. Annie's mouth went dry, and her stomach heaved as though she were going to be sick. She backed away, trying to keep from screaming, but her foot slipped in something sticky.

She regained her feet and looked desperately around the room, which was empty except for a woman in shock, her dead husband, and Annie.

"Help me, Lord," the terrified girl sobbed, as she sat back on her heels, well away from the body. She covered her face with her hands and cried, giving herself over to her fear. Finally, there were no more tears. She had cried herself dry. As she wiped her eyes on the back of her hand, she recalled the words of Psalm 23 and began to say them to herself. When she came to the line, "yea, though I walk through the valley of the shadow of death, I will fear no evil, for thou art with me," her voice trembled. But she felt comforted.

Rising from the floor, she smoothed her hair away from her face and looked with pity at young Mrs. Lesker, now a widow. "Come," she whispered, "we need to go home. I can't carry you, but lean on my shoulder and I'll help you out."

She pulled on Mrs. Lesker's arm until the woman budged from the bed. First coaxing, then pulling, and at times even dragging the judge's wife, Annie managed to get them both out of the house.

By the time they reached the horse, her back ached, and she knew there was no way she could boost the older woman up onto the saddle. Mrs. Letcher seemed to grasp the situation. She held onto the saddle and pulled herself up. Then Annie climbed on in front.

Mrs. Lesker's body seemed so limp that Annie feared she would simply slip off the horse. "You must hold onto me, do you hear?" she asked sharply. The older woman responded by clasping her arms tightly around the girl's waist until Annie began to relax. It was going to be all right.

They walked slowly over the trail that had seemed so pleasant only an hour earlier, with Annie content to let the horse set its own pace. When at last they reached the barn, her eyes filled with tears. God had preserved them. She patted Mrs. Lesker's hand and said, "We're home. You're safe here."

The next several hours were forever blurred in the young woman's memory. She knew that someone helped her from the horse, but she couldn't remember who. She remembered being stripped of her soiled dress, bathed with gentle hands, and given a glass of warm milk to make her sleep.

Neddy told her what happened next, because the rest of the family thought she had suffered enough. It all went back to the war, Neddy said. The British in South Carolina had occupied many towns. But having redcoats in their villages and seeing neighbors befriend the British soldiers had been more than some patriots could bear. They organized raiding parties to attack the British and their Tory helpers. The redcoats fought back, hanging any American raiders whom they caught.

Soon, the South was full of these small, vicious battles. Things grew worse for settlers, Neddy said, as angry Tories, made bold by the presence of the redcoats, no longer felt they had to hide their beliefs. Throughout the South they raided and pillaged. A Tory who had known Judge Lesker all his life, had lurked in the bushes until it was safe to murder. The cruel man had done it while the judge's wife watched terrified from her bed.

The patriots returned swift justice, Neddy announced proudly. They hanged the guilty man in the town square as a warning to other traitors. But the thought of justice did not cheer Annie, who wondered about a war that turned neighbor against neighbor.

Mrs. Lesker slowly regained her strength, but Annie wondered if her friend would ever rejoice again. Only by faith could she believe that God was in charge, even of this awful war.

ON TO RICHMOND

"IF YOU EAT ANY MORE OF THOSE BERRIES, NEDDY Henry, you are going to be sick," Betsy said, speaking through purple lips and wiping her own blue-stained fingers on the apron of her dress.

Neddy, deep in a blueberry thicket, only laughed. "I haven't tasted anything so good since . . ." The boy's memory obviously failed him, as he continued popping the round juicy berries into his mouth faster than he put them in the bucket.

"The mosquitoes are bothering me," Betsy fretted, slapping a large one that had just landed on her arm. "At least they aren't as bad as they were in Williamsburg. Do you remember the mosquitoes there?"

It was late summer, 1780, and the Henrys had been at Leatherwood for a year already. For Neddy, memories of Williamsburg and Scotchtown were fading. "I wouldn't trade Leatherwood for all the Williamsburgs in the world," he proclaimed.

"I would," said Annie, who had been quietly picking berries nearby.

"Oh, Annie. You don't mean that," her brother protested. "You hated all that Williamsburg la di da. You told me so yourself. You said you were never so happy as when you came back to Scotchtown. Didn't you say that?"

"Well, maybe I did. But Scotchtown wasn't Leatherwood," Annie snapped back.

Casting a surprised glance at her sister, Betsy said, "Don't you remember when I complained about Leatherwood that you told me to be content?"

With a great sigh, Annie straightened up and walked out of the thicket. "I'm not saying I'm not content at Leatherwood. I just said that I wouldn't mind being back in Williamsburg."

"Back in Williamsburg, you'd be right in the middle of a war," Betsy reminded her sister.

"Here at Leatherwood, we aren't that far from war," Annie retorted.

The war had gone on five years already, with most of the fighting in the north. Even though there had been no fighting in Virginia since the war's earliest days, the colony shared in the cost of war. Many of the soldiers were Virginians, like Annie's two older brothers, William and

John. Andrew Thacker, a neighbor from Scotchtown, also fought with General Washington.

Virginians had sent more than soldiers. They had provided the army with food and money. Every family in Virginia felt the squeeze as prices rose and food became scarce. It was true that Leatherwood had forests full of game and wild berries. The Henrys had not gone hungry, but now the British army threatened to march through North Carolina and into Virginia. No one was safe from this long, expensive war.

"I bet you Annie has a beau there," Neddy taunted, hoping that she would get angry and maybe chase him.

Betsy giggled, but Annie didn't find it humorous. With an exasperated sigh, she turned and walked toward the house, her heavy bucket dragging at her side.

Behind her Neddy and Betsy continued their teasing. "Who could it be? Let's see, Tom Jefferson is married. How about Mr. Madison? I bet Annie will fall in love with a graybeard like Mr. Lee. Why he's as old as Father." That was enough to set the two youngsters laughing all over again.

Annie turned and glared at them, but they were having too much fun to notice. After leaving the berries at the kitchen, she stomped into the house.

"Annie, is that you?" Dolly asked from her bedroom.

"Yes, ma'am," Annie answered, fearing that she had aroused one of the sleeping children.

"We have a letter today from Sister Woods. Would you come here? I'd like you to read it."

Dolly leaned over a trunk, looking with displeasure at a soiled petticoat. When she heard her stepdaughter's footsteps, she turned, a smile replacing the frown. Tucking a stray brown hair back under her cap, she motioned Annie to one of the chairs, pulling a letter from her apron pocket as she did so.

Annie bent over her aunt's spidery scrawl, trying to make out the words. When she had finished, she looked up at Dolly, who brushed at an invisible spot of dirt on a lace collar. "Poor woman," Annie said finally. "Two little ones to raise alone. I didn't know her husband was so ill."

"Nor did we. Mr. Woods was such a quiet man. He never complained over his ailments."

Dolly continued sorting out clothing from her trunk, clearly not pleased with what she was finding. "Just look at this," she said, holding up an apron with a hole in the middle of it. "Chewed by mice, I imagine. I don't know if anything that I left packed away will be wearable."

"Are you looking for something in particular?" Annie asked, as she joined Dolly near the trunk.

Without looking up from her work, her mother said in a soft voice, "Your father and I thought you might go to Sister Woods and help out for a time. I thought I might find some wearable clothes for you."

For a minute Annie thought she had misunderstood.

Could God really be answering her prayer to leave Leatherwood? "You mean I would go to Richmond?" she asked, trying not to appear too eager.

"Would you mind it terribly?" Dolly asked, looking up for the first time.

Trying not to seem too excited, Annie smiled and said, "If you think I could be helpful, I wouldn't mind going."

Dolly's eyes danced, but she hid her smile behind a handkerchief. Frowning deliberately, she said, "Of course I could send Betsy. . . . She's young, but she is so calming to be around. Don't you agree?"

"Much too young," Annie said more forcefully than she intended. "Besides, I can be every bit as calm as Betsy if that's what the situation requires."

"Would it be a great sacrifice for you?" Dolly asked solemnly. But Annie caught the laughter in her eyes. She threw down the stockings that she held in her hand and said, "You know that I want to go, don't you? Please say yes."

"My only concern for you is safety. But your father says that the British are as likely to attack near Leatherwood as they are to reach Richmond. It makes me sad to say that we can't protect you here. So the answer is yes, you may go," Dolly said. "In fact, you may leave with your father when he goes to the assembly."

Annie turned somber. "I didn't know Father was

going again so soon. He hasn't been home more than a month. I don't want to abandon you."

"You aren't abandoning me," Dolly said. "I'll have plenty of help. In fact, Betsy is devoted to me and the children."

Annie fidgeted nervously, twisting her fingers on her lap and gnawing at her lip. She felt ashamed that she was so eager to leave her family. Dolly reached out a comforting hand. "There's no shame in wanting to start your own life, Annie," she said. "Every bird knows when it is time to leave the nest."

"You know I love you all," Annie said.

"Of course we do. And your father and I agree that it will be good for you to help your father's sister."

After a week's worth of activity, Annie and her father finally set off for Richmond, now the capital of Virginia. They reached the city late on the evening of September 27, 1780. A boy in a tricorner hat rang a bell and called out, "Traitor's plot discovered. Arnold gets away."

Patrick Henry stopped the wagon in the midst of the busy street and beckoned for the newsboy. He scanned the paper eagerly, shaking his head when he had finished the story.

"What is it?" Annie asked, dismayed at the change in her father's expression.

"Benedict Arnold, one of General Washington's favorite and most trusted aides, has turned traitor and joined the British. It is a sad thing," he said. "He tried to betray his command at West Point but was discovered before the plot could hatch."

"Why would he leave now, Father? Does he think we have no chance of winning?"

"I don't know what he is thinking. He married a British girl, and he lost sight of honor. But if he thinks we will abandon the fight against tyranny at this late date, he is mistaken."

Around them the traffic surged forward, as the once-sleepy town bustled with crowds who had business before the assembly. Men and women promenaded down the main street, dressed in their city best. Looking down at her own dusty dress and comparing it to the ones she saw made Annie blush. Turning to her father, who also carried plenty of road dust, she said, "I know it isn't important," Annie said, "but we don't look as though we belong in the city."

Her father chuckled. "We'll take you to your aunt's, and I'll grab a room at the inn. We'll both be able to bathe and put on our city clothes. You wait, Annie. In a matter of days, you'll feel right at home here. Besides, if Richmond ever becomes so much like London that a simple yeoman farmer and his family don't feel fancy enough, then we have already lost the war."

When Annie first met her aunt, she was struck by her physical resemblance to her father. But their appearance was all the brother and sister had in common. She was a dreamy, impractical woman who let her children run around like wild animals throughout her wood frame house. To Annie it didn't seem as though her aunt was really there. Her mind always seemed somewhere else. And the poor cousins, Samuel and Amos, were the most unruly children that Annie had ever met. So starved were they for attention that they constantly misbehaved in order to get it.

At night, when Annie was in the quiet of her own room, she thought with wry amusement about the way God works. At Leatherwood, the young woman had felt crowded by all the people who shared such a small house. She had wanted time alone. In Richmond, she had a room alone. But her waking hours were spent shepherding two rowdy, attention-needing children. Annie found herself missing Betsy and Neddy and the little children. Mostly, though, she missed Dolly, whose calm demeanor had made a crowded house peaceful.

"I will have to learn to be the calm one," Annie told herself. "Right now this house has no loving center, but maybe it can develop one."

She buckled down to the job she had set before her. Each day, the two boys and Annie did an hour of school work. She took them outside for long walks along the river, where they talked to the boat captains. Other times they meandered along the creeks. She showed them how to make fishing poles, something her brothers had been born knowing how to do. She urged her aunt to resume their family Bible readings, and when the widow was too tired, Annie did it herself.

One cold winter day, the boys were begging to go outside.

"It's too cold," she said. "Why don't you make something?"

"Teach us to whittle," pleaded Samuel.

"Me too," Amos, who was only seven, added.

Annie threw up her hands. "I don't know how to whittle. Didn't your father teach you to do these things? My brother Neddy can do it. And he's not much bigger than you. I don't know how he learned. He just watched and did it."

"But who can we watch?" the boys whined.

Annie could teach them to sew, but they wanted nothing to do with "women's work." Finally, not knowing what else to do, she promised that on the first nice day they might walk up to the tavern and see if there would be some men whittling on the porch. Annie rather doubted it, since it was cold.

There came a day in January, 1781, that was so balmy it seemed like spring. "Today is the day, boys," she said to them after she had gone outside to test the weather.

They hurriedly pulled on their overcoats and boots. Soon they were ready to go.

The streets were peaceful. The newspapers warned that British troops were building strength at Yorktown, but that was more than a hundred miles away. No one thought much about it. The tavern was only three blocks away, but the boys were so full of energy after being cooped up that Annie let them run and holler for a while. Finally, each one armed with a pocket knife, they set off for the tavern. The boys pushed at each other until Annie feared they might do danger to themselves or someone else with the little knives they carried.

"Be careful with those knives," she scolded. "No more pushing or shoving."

With relief, she saw that several men were seated on the wooden bench in front of the tavern. Smoke curled from the pipes they held in their teeth, and their bellies strained against the buttons of their vests. The boys scooted over eagerly and positioned themselves where they could watch and listen to the conversation.

"You behave," she admonished them before crossing the street to the milliners, where she hoped to get new ribbons for her bonnet.

The nice weather brought everyone out, and Annie spent a pleasant hour in the store visiting with people she hadn't seen all winter. She occasionally peeked out the window to check up on the boys, who were contentedly carving on their own pieces of wood.

A gnawing in her stomach reminded Annie that it was time for dinner. She opened the door to the milliners and was astonished to see a horde of redcoats coming down the street. The color drained from her face as she watched the black-booted army march down Richmond's main street. Behind her, women gasped and some burst into tears. All up and down the street, shutters slammed shut as the townsfolk hid behind the security of their walls.

All Annie could think about were the young boys across the street. Gathering up her skirts, she ran and grabbed them by the hand. They resisted her. "We want to watch," Samuel said. Annie turned an angry face toward her young wards. They were so impressed by the scarlet jackets, brass buttons, and white breeches, that they couldn't pull their eyes away.

"Hurry. Hurry," she scolded, while pulling on their arms. But they wriggled free of her grasp and began running down the street toward the oncoming soldiers. Annie stood motionless, frozen by fear of what the soldiers might do.

Several grinned and pointed at the boys who were marching alongside the procession. One even put his hat on Samuel's head. Annie trembled with anger at her cousins. What should she do?

Just then, a young man walked up beside her. He was

dressed in a gray vest and black breeches and wore his brownish hair pulled back in a simple pony tail at the neck. He bowed slightly and smiled, while saying softly, "Would you like me to retrieve the little scamps for you?"

Annie looked at him gratefully. "Would you?" she asked. He didn't need any other urging. In an instant, he had swept up beside the marching cousins, pulled one up under each arm, and tossed the redcoat's hat into a mud puddle.

He ignored the protests coming from the boys and the soldier. With a few graceful strides, he returned to Annie's side, still holding the squawking boys by the ears. "You rascals have something to say to the young lady?"

Ducking their chins, they scowled at the pavement until the young man gave their ears a little pinch. "Ouch," they howled, wriggling to get free, but that just made their ears hurt more. Grudgingly, Amos apologized, and the young man let him go. Samuel wiggled a bit longer, but when he saw the determination in the young man's eyes, he relented and apologized.

"Will that do?" the young man asked Annie before loosening his grip. She nodded shyly, wondering why he looked so familiar to her.

"The nerve of the redcoats marching into the capital in all their glory," he muttered as he stared glumly at the passing column of soldiers.

"I'll take these boys home," Annie whispered. "Their

mother will be worried with all the commotion." Annie also was worried. How could the redcoats have taken Richmond without even a shot being fired? "I don't know how I can ever thank you for your help."

The young man bowed slightly. "It was my pleasure. Let me introduce myself. Spencer Roane, at your service."

Annie giggled. That's why he looked so familiar. She had met him in Williamsburg three years before. "I believe we've met," she managed to say after an awkward silence. "My name is Annie Henry."

Now it was Spencer's turn to be surprised. "But you were just a little thing then. I would not have recognized you," he said. "You have grown up."

"I am seventeen," Annie said a bit smugly. "And how is your cousin Grace?"

"As much a pill as ever. Her father has threatened to send her to the Caribbean until she learns to behave," he said shrugging his shoulders.

Just then a high-stepping white horse carrying a scarlet-clad soldier in a plumed hat pranced by. "The traitor Benedict Arnold," Spencer said, his face stony with disapproval. "I mustn't stay here any longer. I may do something I will regret." Impulsively, he grabbed Annie's hand and landed a kiss on it before turning and striding away.

Blushing furiously, she watched his retreating figure until he was out of sight. Next to her, the cousins were nursing their sore ears and bruised egos, casting gloomy looks at her.

"You'll not tell Mother?" Amos pleaded.

"She wouldn't care," Samuel said with a note of belligerence.

"But she'd care if Annie got angry and went away," Amos retorted.

"I'm not going anywhere," Annie said sternly. "I made a promise to your mother and my parents that I would come help. But you boys must learn to obey."

"Why must we?" Samuel asked saucily.

"Because your life will be full of trouble if you don't. God won't abide a rebellious spirit."

Taking aim, the boy kicked a rock with the toe of his well-scuffed boot. When they reached the unassuming house where they lived, Amos scampered up the stairs, but Samuel refused to go in. Annie left him staring moodily at the soldiers who now filled the streets.

REDCOATS

THROUGHOUT THE NIGHT, GUNSHOTS SHATTERED the silence. An explosion sent flames soaring into the heavens. Smaller fires burned here and there, and their acrid smoke filled the air. Annie paced nervously in her room, wishing she were back in Leatherwood. Where was General Washington's army?

Bonfires burned in the streets and drunken soldiers danced on the sidewalks. Tory sympathizers, who had hidden their admiration for the king out of fear, now celebrated with the red-coated conquerors.

Sitting in her dark room, lit only by a candle, Annie dashed off a letter to her parents. Tomorrow she would take it to the post office. It was impossible to sleep with all the noise and confusion. At any moment, soldiers could be pounding at her aunt's door.

Morning came and found Annie slumped down in a

chair, her head drooping awkwardly on her chest. She woke with a groan. After stretching her stiff muscles, she glanced at the desk.

Her letter was there as a reminder that she would have to go out to the post office.

She opened the shuttered window. Outside on her aunt's sidewalk lay two soldiers wrapped in blankets. All up and down the street, the soldiers littered the ground like so many red statues. "They aren't even in a camp," Annie muttered with disgust. "It's as though Benedict Arnold wants to soil the entire town with his British friends."

Annie feared that the presence of the British meant that General Washington was losing the war. She hurriedly washed and pulled on her dress, eager to go down the street and hear some gossip.

Her aunt was drinking tea in the parlor. Her face was pale, and Annie could see that she had not slept well either. "What is the matter, Aunty?" Annie asked.

"I looked in on the boys. Amos is sleeping like a darling. But Samuel's bed is empty. I've searched the house, but he isn't to be found." Then looking down with a shamefaced expression, she added, "I'm afraid to go outside. Those soldiers are so intimidating."

Annie looked at her aunt with pity. "I'll go," she said brusquely.

Her aunt watched as Annie pulled on a long woolen

cape and tied her calash under her chin. "You aren't afraid of anything, are you?" she asked.

Annie stared at her aunt in astonishment. "I'm frightened of all sorts of things," she said. "It is only by the grace of God that I have courage, if that's what it is."

"With Samuel, it isn't courage. It's impulsiveness. I fear that he may do something foolish because he doesn't think. And he is very angry."

Again Annie was surprised. She hadn't thought her aunt paid any attention to the boys. The girl hesitated at the door, wanting to say something to comfort her anxious aunt. "I think I understand Samuel," she said. "I felt awfully angry when my mother died. I did some foolish things, just like Samuel is doing. It wasn't until I learned the Gospel—that Christ the Son of God died for me— that I put away the anger."

But from her aunt's wooden expression, it was hard to know if she understood.

The cold air put color in Annie's cheeks as she hurried through the streets, keeping her face turned to the ground. Here and there she saw from the corner of her eye other residents rushing along the sidewalks, being careful not to come too close to any of the soldiers. It was as if all the people in Richmond believed that if they stared at the ground, they would be invisible. Smoke continued rising from a building at the far end of town. With anger, she saw that several other storefronts had been burned.

Outside the post office was a red-coated officer. Whenever anyone went in to mail a letter, he examined the address. Annie hesitated. It would not be wise to let that British soldier see that she was writing to Patrick Henry at Leatherwood.

Across the street, a small band of men had gathered. They ignored the pointed looks cast in their direction by the post office guard. Annie slipped over so that she could hear what they were saying. "The legislature has moved to Charlottesville," she heard one man say.

"The British would like nothing better than to catch the legislature—maybe Governor Jefferson, as well."

"Those men would never let themselves fall into British hands," another man answered. "They're too wily for that."

Annie wanted to ask about her father, but looking around the group and seeing all the strange faces, she suddenly grew suspicious. How did she know they weren't spies? The Tories in Richmond would be rejoicing at the presence of the redcoats. And why weren't the soldiers breaking up this group?

Before she could decide, she felt a tap on her shoulder. Turning, she saw Spencer Roane, who looked at her quizzically.

"Are you sure it is safe to be out this morning?" he asked while guiding her beyond the hearing of the crowd.

"I thought I would hasten out to find the news," she said. "But my cousin Samuel, the stubborn one, is missing. He left sometime during the night, and my aunt is crazy with worry over him. I am trying to find him." She looked into Spencer Roane's sympathetic face and felt a lifting of the burden. "If you were a young boy of eight, where would you hide?" she asked.

"I would have been in a barn with the horses," he said with a laugh. "I always liked a good horse."

"Well Samuel has no horses," Annie said, chewing her lip. "He seemed to like the soldiers, and that is what has me worried. Would he be with the British? Is there a camp?"

At the mention of the soldiers, Spencer's face darkened. His eyes looked moodily off into the distance. "Their camp is down the road," he said, pointing off behind her. "But they didn't bother sleeping there last night," he said.

"Do you think Samuel would go there?" Annie asked with a growing sense of excitement mixed with dread.

"I guess it might be a likely place," he admitted. "But it isn't a safe place." Then nodding at the cluster of men behind her, he said, "The streets are not safe either. If one of these soldiers were to discover your identity, they would likely take you prisoner. Don't trust anyone, unless you know for certain that they are loyal to the cause."

Annie looked back at the soldier at the post office, glad that she had had the good sense not to mail her letter. But her hopes for her young cousin withered. "What shall I do?" she asked, feeling dangerously close to tears.

"Don't you worry," the young man said gently. "I will go to the camp myself. If I see the scamp, I will bring him directly to your aunt's home."

A broad smile lit Annie's face. "You are so kind to me," she said gratefully. "I will wait for you there."

It was three hours later that Spencer Roane returned with a mutinous Samuel in tow. After reuniting the boy with his worried mother, Annie sat in the parlor with the young man while he recounted his story.

Spencer sipped from his steaming mug of cider and stretched his long legs out on the hooked rug that covered the floor. "Just as you thought, the boy was in the camp. He was dressed like a redcoat from head to toe and was dancing to the fife. The men were having great fun at his expense, but he didn't mind. The more they joshed him, the more he danced."

"How awful," Annie said, closing her eyes and covering her face with her hands. "Just think what they would have done if they had known who he was."

Spencer Roane grew serious, though he couldn't completely extinguish the amusement in his eyes. "I'm afraid they did know. He told everyone his name, and when that didn't get any attention, he told them he was Patrick Henry's nephew. That brought even Benedict Arnold out of his tent."

Annie blushed a deep crimson. "That little . . . I'd like to strangle him."

"I'm afraid I beat you to it. He heard quite a lecture on loving family and country while I accompanied him home. I even told him how Doc Withers had his eyes gouged out for consorting with the enemy. I think it made an impression."

Annie nodded. "I appreciate that," she said. "His mother is too soft on him, and I don't really have any authority."

Spencer emptied his mug and rose reluctantly from his chair. "I would like to stay and visit," he admitted. "Perhaps when the present trouble is gone from our doorsteps you would allow me to call."

Blushing furiously, Annie nodded. As she watched the dark-haired fellow stroll down the street, she threw up her hands in disgust. *Why can't I be more like Betsy?* she thought.

Later that week Annie walked to the apothecary to get some medicine for her aunt. She was waiting at the counter when suddenly, from the street outside the shop, came the sound of wild snorting, loud laughter, and screams. Looking out the door, she saw a herd of pigs running crazily from gutter to gutter, as if they didn't know which way to go. Other pigs spun in circles like tops, as they chased their own curly tails. Behind them, a mob of Redcoats waved their hats, which only drove the pigs into a greater state of confusion.

Annie stepped back as a huge swine crashed into the door before dizzily stumbling back into the street. A few children chased the tiny ones, while their mothers tried to get out of the way as the crazy animals plowed through the town.

Across the street, the tavern door opened and a whisky cask came rolling into the street. From its side flowed a trail of liquor. As the barrel wobbled into the street, the pigs chased it, greedily slurping up the liquid. Like dogs madly chasing a bone, the meaty beasts lunged after the barrel, snorting nastily at any pig that got in the way.

The first cask was followed by another, and another, as the redcoats went through the tavern's supply of ale and whisky, ripping open the sides of each cask before sending it spinning out into the street where the now-drunken pigs awaited. The smell of the sour liquid filled the air, and Annie looked with disgust at the pigs who now wobbled on unsteady legs after the casks.

She felt her temper rise. Without thinking, she pushed the door open ready to march across the street to find an officer to discipline his troops. Three steps out the door, she turned and stumbled over a pig that had fallen down drunk in the middle of the street. She caught her balance, but then proceeded to plop her foot right in the middle of a whisky puddle, splashing the sour liquid onto her dress.

Across the street, soldiers laughed, but none came to her assistance. With disgust mixed with embarrassment, she tossed her head as she turned back toward the apothecary. A voice behind her said, "Excuse my men. They have been fighting a long time and have lost their manners."

Annie turned to see a proud-looking man with mocking eyes staring at her, his lip curled in amusement at her distress. With a flourish, he doffed his plumed hat and made an exaggerated bow. "General Benedict Arnold," he said hautily.

Annie fixed her angry eyes on him and said, "I've always wondered what a traitor looked like. Now I know." She turned away, but the general grabbed her arm angrily.

"You are talking to a general in His Majesty's Army. You must show respect."

Annie raised her chin defiantly. "I will show respect to my God, to my parents, and to the rightful leaders of my country. You are none of those things. And a king who would allow himself to be represented by soldiers who carry on like this is not worthy of respect."

Pulling her arm away, Annie stalked away from the

general, leaving him standing in angry astonishment. Before he could recover his composure, she was in the apothecary, surrounded by her patriot neighbors. He glared at her through the glass, before turning and marching across the street with a look that silenced the high spirits of his troops. In a sharp voice, he gave orders for them to assemble. Then as suddenly as they had marched into town, they marched back toward their camp, leaving behind the smoldering remains of burnt buildings, charred bonfires, broken casks, and drunken pigs.

SPENCER ROANE

IN APRIL, BENEDICT ARNOLD AGAIN SENT HIS RAIDERS into Richmond. They found little of value, especially since the legislature no longer met there. One day the boys went with their mother on a visit to some friends in the country. For Annie, it marked nearly a year since she had moved from Leatherwood to Richmond. Seeing that the day was warm and the sky clear, she packed a picnic lunch and carried it down to the river bank to eat.

The water lapped peacefully at the shore. As she gazed at the river, Annie watched gulls swooping low over the water, sometimes plunging their beaks beneath its glittery surface and coming up with a fish.

Lying back on the grassy slope, she watched the powdery clouds float by and remembered a picnic at the creek at Scotchtown when she had first met Andrew Thacker. Even now she could hear his fife playing in her imagination. Andrew, like her brothers John and William, had gone to be a soldier. She wondered wistfully if he had found it as exciting as he thought it would be. Had he been injured, maybe even killed? She hadn't heard a thing.

Annie found herself sinking into a melancholy mood as she considered her past and the sweet hopes she had nursed of freedom in a new country. All the violence at Leatherwood and Benedict Arnold's army had destroyed those hopes. Now she prayed only that her brothers would come home safely. What a waste if they should die and Virginia still be in bondage to the king. Annie shut her eyes against the dismal thought and prayed.

As she lay there praying, she heard a rustling next to her. Opening her eyes, she found Spencer Roane gazing at her so intensely that it made her blush and hurry to sit up. Embarrassed at being caught staring, he turned his eyes and looked out over the water.

"The housekeeper told me that I might find you here," he said. "I hope I'm not intruding."

"Not at all," she answered as she busied her nervous fingers with a fold in her skirt.

Silence followed this brief exchange, as both were suddenly tongue-tied. Finally, Spencer recalled why he had come. He pulled an envelope out of his pocket and handed it to Annie. "I brought this from your father," he said. "I thought you would want to read it right away."

Annie examined the letter. "Have you recently seen

Father?" she asked curiously, turning the envelope over in her hand as though looking for a clue. Several curly hairs sprang out from under her white cap and fell over her eyes, but the girl seemed not to notice.

Spencer reached out and brushed the curls gently back. His gesture startled Annie, who pulled away. "Excuse me, I don't know what I was doing. . . ." he stammered. "Those curls were just so distracting," he added in a small voice.

Annie's heart beat rapidly. She felt hot and wished she had chosen a shadier place for her picnic lunch.

"Go ahead. Open the letter. I won't find it rude," the young man said, seeing her discomfort and knowing he had contributed to it.

She slipped her finger under the flap and pulled open the seal. "Shall I read it out loud to you?" she asked shyly.

"I would love to hear it," he answered.

Dear Annie,

I trust Sister Woods is well and believe that you are proving to be a help to her. I write to let you know that the folks at Leatherwood are fine, although the British Army came close and threatened to enter Virginia through North Carolina. Had they done so, we might have been close to the fighting.

As you know, the assembly has been meeting without incident in Charlottesville, where we expected to be well out of the way of any trouble. Several nights ago, however, a young captain, Jack Jouett, overheard General Cornwallis ordering 250 cavalrymen to Charlottesville in order to overtake us. Had the plot been successful, I, along with my fellow legislators, Governor Jefferson, and other state officials would have all been captured. What a blow to the cause it would have been!

Jouett rode all night and warned the assembly. We immediately rose from our beds and made haste for Staunton in the Blue Ridge. I traveled with John Tyler, Speaker Harrison, and your uncle William Christian. We didn't dare stop, not knowing how far behind us the British cavalry were. (We later learned that they had stopped for breakfast, but we didn't know it at the time.)

On we scrambled through the dark night and into the next morning, until we could go no further. Tired and hungry, we decided to stop at a little cabin hidden in a mountain gorge. It was visible to us only by a tiny wisp of smoke that rose above the rocky summit.

An old woman answered the door and peered out suspiciously. "Who are you? Where have you come from?" she asked. I stood near the back, not wanting to draw attention to myself. Old Tyler said we were members of the legislature fleeing from the British cavalry.

"Ride on then, you cowardly knaves," she cackled, waving a broom at us as though we were chaff which she personally was going to sweep away.

I pushed forward and tried to reason with her, vainly I might add. Tyler interrupted me as I spoke. "What would you say if I told you that Patrick Henry fled with the rest of us?" he asked her.

She glared at him with a look I wouldn't want to see again. It made me tremble in my boots. (How glad I am that your mother Dolly is a gentle soul. You must follow her example when you marry. A husband is more likely to be won with kindness.)

When Annie read those words, she blushed because of the young man next to her. Taking a deep breath, she began to read again.

"Patrick Henry?" she asked in amazement. "I would tell you there wasn't a word of truth in it." She harumphed and shook her broom until all four of us almost turned and ran. "Why, Patrick Henry would never do such a cowardly thing."

I almost died laughing when I heard those words. Here she had me trembling with fear and yet she was holding me up as a paragon of bravery. That's when the fun began. Tyler pointed at me and said, "But this is Mr. Henry."

The old woman demanded that I go inside and stand by the fire so that she could get a better look at me. Seeing something in my face that she liked, she finally relented, saying, "Well then, if that is Patrick Henry, it must be all right."

Next thing I knew we were sitting in her warm parlor, toasting comfortably in front of the fire, sipping warm cider and eating corn bread. Afterwards we all had a good laugh over the story.

We are now in Staunton, far from trouble. I know about Benedict Arnold in Richmond. Don't let it worry you. And don't let yourself be discouraged by concentrating only on the things you see around you. It is a much bigger world than you imagine, and much goes on that you don't know. Trust God.

I am giving this letter into the hand of Spencer Roane, who assisted some of our legislators in their flight to Staunton. Some of us aren't young and can't hazard the journey on horseback. Mr. Roane secured carriages and drove some of the men. Thank him for me.

Your faithful and loving father,

Patrick Henry

Annie looked up from the letter and caught a glimpse of humor in Spencer's eyes. With a smile she said, "Father must have enjoyed the scolding by the old woman. I wouldn't be surprised if he didn't invite her for dinner someday."

"Your father is a marvelous man," Spencer said.

"I think he is. He has convictions that he lives by. And

he is well-loved by his family and his neighbors. That's important, don't you think?"

"Most men expect to be loved by their families," the young man mused. "It seems almost like part of the package. But to be loved, as your father is, by all the yeoman farmers of the state—that is a marvelous thing."

Annie felt herself beaming at the kind words directed at her father. Carefully tucking the letter into her pocket, she turned toward the picnic basket. "Would you eat with me?" she asked him, wanting very much for him to stay.

He hesitated just long enough for her to feel uneasy, as though perhaps he had someplace else to be. Forcing herself to smile, she said, "Go if you must. I didn't mean to detain you so long, for I know how busy you must be. I only wanted to carry out my father's wishes that I thank you for your kindness to his friends and colleagues."

"Is that really all, Annie?" he asked her, looking at her with such tenderness that she forgot the question. His eyes caught hers. For several minutes they sat that way, neither one able or willing to break away. Finally, the young man stood up. "I must go, Annie," he said in a gruff voice. "I would feel less than a gentleman if I were to speak my feelings for you before I had asked your father's permission. Please forgive me for being forward."

With a slight bow, he excused himself and walked

away, leaving Annie sitting on the grassy slope feeling breathless and not sure what she was feeling.

"I think it must be love," she whispered to herself after a moment.

A REUNION

THROUGHOUT THE SPRING OF 1781, BENEDICT ARNOLD and his men pillaged the Virginia countryside, setting fires to the storehouses filled with grain and tobacco.

General Washington was eager to capture the famous traitor, so he sent the French General Lafayette, with 1,200 men in pursuit of the dangerous Arnold. When Lafayette and his men reached Virginia, however, the British recalled Arnold to New York. The raiding continued, now under the orders of the British General Cornwallis.

Annie learned not to despair. Though the news from Virginia was bad, there had been reports of American victories at Kings Meadow and Cowpens in North Carolina. Didn't her father tell her not to judge things based only on what she could see?

One day in October, 1781, Annie's quiet world

erupted. She received a letter from her brother William telling her that John was very sick. During a hurried march with General Washington's army from New York to Yorktown, east of Williamsburg on the peninsula, John had taken sick with the flu. High fever and chills had made him unfit for fighting, and the army had abandoned him in Williamsburg. Would Annie go to him? William pleaded.

If the situation hadn't been so grave, Annie would have found it amusing. Once again she was being sent off as nurse and comforter to the sick. It wasn't a role that she would have predicted for herself even a year earlier. But people asked for her, and she was glad to go. So many times in the past someone else had comforted her. Now it was her turn.

Her aunt sent her off tearfully. "You've been a balm to my family," she said. "We would not have survived the past year without your gentle love and patience."

The words startled Annie. How she had longed to have Dolly's grace, and now her aunt seemed to suggest that she had a touch of it. Had God done that? She took the basket of food and medicine her aunt offered, before turning to say good-bye to her young cousins. It grieved her to part with Amos and Samuel. The younger one clung to her and begged her to stay. But Samuel was too old for tears and begging. Unnoticed by his mother and brother, he slipped an ink-blotched note into Annie's hand as she climbed into the coach that would carry her to Williamsburg.

She watched them grow tiny through teary eyes as the carriage lumbered along the dusty track toward the coast. When they were no longer in sight, she opened the grubby piece of paper.

"I love you," it read in Samuel's childish script. "And God loves me."

Annie smiled as she folded the little letter and put it back in her pocket. Many nights she had spent reading the family Bible to the willful child, despairing that its healing words would ever touch his stubborn heart. Maybe he had heard more than she thought.

She dozed away the hours and didn't wake until they reached the town. She watched out the window as they rolled into the familiar city, where she had spent so much time in the Governor's Palace. The town was virtually empty now. Many people had moved with the capital to Richmond. Those who had stayed behind had been hard hit by the war. Many shops were closed, and the streets seemed nearly deserted.

The coach dropped Annie at the Wythes' house, where her friend Kate Marsh still lived. The Wythes, like so many others, had abandoned Williamsburg to be farther away from danger, but they had left servants there to protect their house and property.

Annie stood hesitantly on the stoop, letting the memories flood back. Before she could knock, the door opened. Kate clapped her hands and tugged Annie inside. "Don't stand outside gathering moss," she laughed.

Annie smiled at the friend she hadn't seen for three years. She had blossomed. She no longer had the frail skittish look that had so provoked Grace to tease her. Now she radiated an inner calm that made her plain features seem beautiful.

"I know you feel dusty and dirty. Those coaches are awful, aren't they? I hope you didn't travel with any unpleasant people." A worried expression crossed Kate's brow.

"It wasn't so awfully bad," Annie said. "But it seemed long, since I was worrying about John. Do you know how he is?"

"That is one of the surprises that I have for you," Kate said with a smile. "He's upstairs in one of the bedrooms. I went to the infirmary and claimed him. We've been taking good care of him, but he seems dreadfully lonely for his family."

Annie threw her arms around her friend. "You are good," she said. "May I go to see him now?"

"Even before you bathe?" Kate asked.

"I couldn't wait a minute, now that I know he is here," Annie confessed. "I'll have a good wash after I've seen him."

She found her brother sleeping fitfully in a tall four-poster bed. He had kicked off his sheets, so she remade the bed, pulling the sheets up over him. While she worked, she studied his face. Her brother no longer bore a look of innocent mischief. His cheekbones jutted out of a gaunt, colorless face.

John looked so altered that it almost broke Annie's heart to see him. She turned away from the bed, her eyes full of tears, as she realized how hard the war had been for General Washington's soldiers.

Grace met her on the stairs. After taking one look at Annie's sad face, she wrapped her arms around her. "He looks bad, I know. But the fever is getting better. You'll see, once he's back on the farm, he'll be a new man."

Sighing deeply, Annie said, "He looks so much like my father. It's troubling, for he isn't yet twenty—and he looks like an old man. Has everyone who has gone to be a soldier come back like that?"

"Not at all. Some are wounded in their bodies. But others, like John, seem to be more wounded in their minds. He is sick, but he also is so dreadfully sad. I think it will take awhile for him to get over the things he has seen."

By now the two young ladies were seated in the parlor, where Kate had brought a warming cup of herb tea to Annie. Despite the sad conversation, Kate seemed so bubbling with happiness that Annie couldn't keep from noticing. "What makes you so happy during this sad time?" she asked, setting her cup down.

"I wanted to tell you before," Kate said with a modest smile. "I'm married. Have been since last month. My name is not Kate Marsh, but Kate Wigglesworth, if you can imagine."

"Married!" Annie looked at her friend with new eyes. There were so many questions she wanted to ask, but they all became tangled up before she could ask them.

Kate's smile froze. "Aren't you happy for me?" she asked in a small voice that reminded Annie of the timid girl her friend had once been.

"Happy? Of course I'm happy. Only there's so much to ask, and I just don't know where to begin."

"His name is William, though I call him Bill," Kate said. "He's a glassblower, and he's trying to earn enough money to buy land out West. Maybe in Kentucky."

Annie listened, thinking about marriage and plans. She thought of Spencer Roane's words and smiled.

To Annie's joy, John did get better. Although he sometimes sank into a melancholy mood, for the most part he was cheerful, waiting quietly on the porch for the women to bring him food or drink or medicine. Annie didn't think she had ever seen her brother be so patient, and it worried her a bit. She longed to see a little of his old spark, but it wasn't to be found.

At night, John and Bill smoked their pipes on the porch and talked of the war. Annie and Kate often joined them and listened as John described what he had seen.

Winters in the North had been brutal, particularly for the southern soldiers who didn't even own the warm coats that their northern comrades had. Food was scarce. One hardtack biscuit sometimes had to last for days before a new supply of grain and meat would reach the troops.

This last march, though, had been more than John's body could take. For weeks General Washington had moved the troops here and there near New York, trying to convince the British that he was going to attack Manhattan Island. Having confused the British thoroughly, Washington ordered his troops to begin the long march south, leaving behind only enough soldiers to fool the British, who thought Washington's entire army was still in New York.

Throughout the sweltering August days the army marched, despite the heat and lack of food. It was an orderly march, John said. Most of the soldiers were veterans of many battles. They were joined by a large army of French soldiers who had promised to fight with the patriots.

By September, the early columns had reached the mouth of the Chesapeake Bay. They loaded onto boats and began the trip to Williamsburg. That's when John had taken sick. Now it was October, and in Yorktown, just a little east of Williamsburg, a major battle was developing.

☆

"Go see William's shop," Kate said one brisk October day when Annie seemed restless. She agreed and walked down to his little glass factory. It was a brick building, open on one side, where a blazing hot fire burned within an enormous furnace. Unlike most open fireplaces, this furnace had a door that closed. Inside was a vat of glowing orange liquid glass.

William stood in front of the furnace, his rotund belly straining against his vest buttons. Though it was cool outside, he wore only a vest and muslin shirt. Sweat streaked down his face. Annie entered the shop just as he donned large leather gloves and scooped up a ball of molten glass on the end of a long iron rod that he held in his hand.

He sat down and rolled the iron bar on his bench. Under his skillful hands, the glass was changed from a rough glob to a smooth ball. When he was satisfied, he blew into the end of the tube and the glass ball expanded, becoming hollow inside. He rolled it and swung it, and the glass ball changed into a vase before her eyes.

Annie was so absorbed in what he was doing that she didn't hear a man run up behind her. Only when he spoke, did she turn to see who it was. "William, could you spare some time?" he gasped. "Thomas was to take food to the troops outside Yorktown, but he is sick and unable to go. There aren't many young men available, but I thought you might be willing."

William wiped his brow on the sleeve of his muslin shirt. He removed the large gloves and set them on his table. Glancing quickly at Annie, he said gruffly, "I'll go. There isn't any work here that won't wait until tomorrow."

"The wagon is loaded at the cooper's. Should I tell them you are coming?"

"Tell them I'll come after I've said good-bye to Kate. You can spare me that time."

Bill and Annie walked back to the Wythes' together. "Will it be dangerous?" Annie asked.

"Not at all," William answered. "I hear the British are trapped in Yorktown. Our army stands between us and them. So I won't even cross enemy lines. There has been traffic back and forth all month."

Annie chewed her lip. "Do you think I could come?" she blurted. "Maybe I'll catch sight of William. I'd like to give him news about John."

Bill scowled, but behind the gruff expression, Annie thought she saw sympathy in his eyes. With a shrug, he said, "I'll ask Kate. If she says it is proper, then I wouldn't mind the company."

Kate didn't like the idea, Annie could tell. Turning to her husband with a sigh of exasperation, she said, "William, take good care of her. Don't let her out of your sight."

He promised, and Annie promised to be good. With

those assurances, Kate sent them off with a basket of food for the journey.

Throughout the ride, they heard the unceasing sound of distant cannon. "Must be 100 guns," Bill muttered. "Hope they belong to us."

When they passed a wagon going the other way, he stopped the driver for news. "How goes the battle?" he asked.

"The patriots are shelling the British. They'll not be able to hang on much longer," the man answered.

Annie allowed herself to smile. Now if only William were out of harm's way. When they reached Yorktown, dense smoke hung over the field. Its smell greeted them long before they could see the cannons that produced it. William drove the wagon to the high ridge where the patriots had set up camp and unloaded the wagon while Annie waited. From their vantage point they could see over the whole field. Arrayed before them were the blue jackets of the colonials, across the field, the scarlet of the British.

William had been right. There were nearly 100 cannon keeping up a constant barrage against the British lines. The gunners paused only to let the smoke clear so they could better see their targets.

During one such pause, as the smoke drifted away, there was movement on the British side. A small figure walked to a high perch and stood at attention. With all eyes focused his way, he began drumming. At first the beats came slow and soft. Then faster and louder. "What does it mean?" Annie asked the big man who stood next to her.

"I think it means parley," he answered. "The British are asking for a meeting."

"Then it is good news," Annie said, her face brightening with hope.

As they waited for the official word, a fifer began to play, and thousands of voices joined to sing, "Yankee Doodle."

"Let's go closer," Annie begged. Together they ran toward the assembled army. They found themselves surrounded by jubilant soldiers who sent thousands of hats into the air as the buoyant sound of "Yankee Doodle" played.

Annie grinned as she heard whispers and then shouts of "Huzzah, they've surrendered."

"Did you hear that, Bill?" she screamed, trying to be heard over the soldiers who crowded around. Though Annie tried to keep her friend in sight, the pushing and jostling of the crowd soon separated them, and she found herself concentrating on not falling. Just then, someone shoved her, and she fell backward into a soldier.

"Are you all right?" the young man asked as he helped her regain her balance.

Embarrassed by her clumsiness, Annie stared at the

ground and began apologizing. "Excuse me," she said before a voice interrupted her.

"Annie? Is that you?"

When she looked up, she recognized her friend from Hanover. "Andrew," she exclaimed.

Before she could hug him, he backed away stammering, "Wait here . . . I can't believe my eyes. . . . Don't you move, you hear. . . ." He rushed off, looking over his shoulder as if to make sure she wouldn't disappear. Within minutes he was back, dragging a dirty soldier behind him.

"William?" Annie asked hesitantly, scarcely recognizing the powder-smeared soldier as her brother.

"Annie Henry. What a sight you are," he said, swallowing her up in a big bear hug. Over his shoulder, Annie saw Andrew Thacker looking wistfully on. Giggling, she pulled away from her brother long enough to plant a kiss on Andrew's cheek. From across the field came the first notes of a mournful tune.

"What are they playing?" Annie asked softly.

"It's a lament," her brother answered. "It's called 'The World Turned Upside Down.' Listen to the words." As the singing from the patriot side subsided, the forlorn words sung by the British hung in the air. "If buttercups buzzed after the bees. If boats were on land, churches on seas . . . the World turned upside down."

"Is the war over?" she asked Kate's husband.

"If the British surrender here, then the war will surely be over," Bill promised.

"And the boys can come home?" she asked.

With huge smiles on their gaunt faces they agreed. "Yes! We will come home."

Annie felt she might burst with happiness. At long last the war seemed to be coming to an end. Freedom was won. Love beckoned. Surely God is good!

HISTORICAL NOTE

ALTHOUGH THESE STORIES ARE FICTION, PATRICK Henry did have a daughter named Annie. She married Spencer Roane on September 7, 1786. Together they had six children. She died in 1799, the same year as her father.

Patrick Henry was elected governor again in 1784. He and his second wife, Dolly, had ten children. He spent the last years of his life happily retired on a farm called Red Hill, where he read the Bible and played with his young family.

Many of the incidents in this book are true. The famous traitor Benedict Arnold did invade Richmond, burn the city, and tear open the liquor casks so that drunken pigs ran wild in the streets. Judge Lesker was murdered in his house while his wife watched from a nearby bed. Patrick Henry did barely escape ahead of the

British cavalry led by Colonel Tarleton, a British soldier famed for his excessive cruelty.

Following is a letter that Patrick Henry wrote to Annie on the occasion of her wedding:

My Dear Daughter:

You have just entered into that state which is replete with happiness or misery.

You are allied to a man of honor, of talents, and of an open, generous disposition. You have, therefore, in your power all the essential ingredients of that system of conduct which you ought invariably to pursue—if you will now see clearly the path from which you will resolve never to deviate.

The first maxim which you should impress upon your mind is never to attempt to control your husband, by opposition, by displeasure, or any other work of anger. . . . Little things that in reality are mere trifles in themselves, often produce bickerings and even quarrels. Never permit them to be a subject of dispute; yield them with pleasure, with a smile of affection. . . .

Cultivate your mind by the perusal of those books which instruct while they amuse. Do not devote much of your time to novels. . . . History, geography, poetry, moral essays, biography, travels, sermons, and other well-written religious productions will not fail to enlarge your understanding, to render you a more agreeable companion, and to exalt your virtue.

Mutual politeness between the most intimate friends is essential to that harmony which should never be broken or interrupted. How important, then, it is between man and wife! . . . I will add that matrimonial happiness does not depend on wealth; no, it is not to be found in wealth, but in minds properly tempered and united to our respective situations.

In the management of your domestic concerns let prudence and wise economy prevail. Unite liberality with a just frugality; always reserve something for the hand of charity; and never let your door be closed to the voice of suffering humanity.